On Page 5 of A KEY TO THE SUITE:

> You will meet Hubbard, a corporation hatchetman on his way to an industry convention with the lousy job of making a report that will toss a man and his family out in the street.

On Page 35 of A KEY TO THE SUITE:

> You will see the efficient hiring of a C-note call girl and watch her plan the hideous scheme to smear Hubbard that will trap him like a snail in a bucket of salt.

On Page 51 of A KEY TO THE SUITE:

> You will witness the inside scenes of a modern Sodom—cheating husbands away on convention, turned a little mad by too much booze and women too willing . . . ambitious wives ready to sell out as much as necessary to insure their husbands' jobs.

And on Page 126 . . .

> A climax of tension and suspense and violence that will convince you the 25 million people who have bought more than 46 MacDonald thrillers know what they're doing. . .

JOHN D. MacDONALD

A KEY TO THE SUITE

FAWCETT GOLD MEDAL • NEW YORK

A KEY TO THE SUITE

Published by Fawcett Gold Medal Books, a unit of CBS Publications, the Consumer Publishing Division of CBS Inc.

ISBN: 0-449-13995-6

Printed in the United States of America

21 20 19 18 17 16 15 14 13 12

One

THE gentle hand of a girl pressed him awake, and he looked up along a tailored arm at the gloriously empty smile of a stewardess. "Fasten your seat belt, please."

When he straightened in the seat and began to grope for the ends of the belt, she resumed her tour of inspection, looking from side to side, waking other sleepers.

It would have to be a surgical technique, he decided. Their smiles are all too alike. A few minutes of deftness with the scalpel, cutting the frown muscles loose, rehooking the nerve circuits, and you would limit each of them to just two expressions—the habitual superior blandness or the dazzling smile. Perhaps with true corporate efficiency they had hooked the smile to the vocal nerve complex so that they could not speak without smiling. "Prepare for ditching," would be said with the same smile as, "How would you like your fillet, sir?"

But of course they had not yet been able to do anything about the expression of the eyes. They all looked at you with the same aseptic, merciless disdain, then walked away, germless Dynel hair a-bounce under the trig cap, tennis hips swinging the military worsted skirts, any bounce of breasts falling neatly within the maximum and minimum allowable limits as set by the airline.

He ran the pad of his thumb down the line of his jaw, feeling the sandstone texture of the night growth of beard, and smacked his lips in self-disgust at the stale and clotted taste in his mouth. He was on the starboard side of the airplane, behind the wings, and as it tilted into the landing pattern, he looked out the port windows and saw the dawn jumble of the city, with random neon still on, paling in the grayness, and the shining eyes of some small cars in the small streets.

The airplane slowed as the flaps were extended, and it felt tentative and less airworthy under him, so that he inadvertently tightened his buttock muscles and held his chest a little higher.

There had been so much jet travel in this past year, a Super-Constellation felt like a flapping silly thing, rough and haphazard, like an old lady roller skating on cobblestones. An intrusion of history, he thought, to ride in this sister of the Ford Tri-motor, and to be killed in one would have certain ludicrous overtones.

"Snob," he said to himself. Fanciful snob at that, with the analysis of surgical smiles, and preference for dying up-to-date—but always fanciful when overtired, always that half step to one side of reality, so the world bulges into strange shapes.

He saw, to the east, a dark gray velvet sea with a pink rim, delicate as porcelain, and then looked down at the racing, upcoming ribbon of warehouses, scrubby lots, auto dumps; then saw the landing strip lights, and tucked his anus up yet more firmly until he felt the yelp of tires, the second contact, the rolling that began to slow down. Then the muscles softened, and he unlatched the safety belt and stifled the sigh that meant—"Hubbard, you made it again." Hubbard, the hero of progress. He remembered being told that when his grandfather bought a battery flashlight and brought it home, they made him go out into the yard to light it up. Dangers have become more joyless. Each horseless carriage shall be proceeded by a man on horseback carrying a red flag by day and a lighted lantern by night.

He retrieved his hat and dispatch case from the overhead shelf and walked down the stairway on wheels into a curious damp warmth like that of a team lockerroom a little while after the last hot shower has been taken. There were puddles on the ramp from recent rain. He marched with the others down an endless corridor, thinking that the air age is turning us into a race of pedestrians.

The main part of the terminal was so savagely airconditioned he felt chilled when the sweat of walking began an immediate evaporation. He found a men's room, whitely lighted, and as he was washing his hands he stared dispassionately at himself in the mirror and was mildly astonished he should look so tidy in that cruel light. The smut-shadow of beard gave him somewhat the look of imported syndicate muscle, but, he decided, of the upper echelon where the payoff goes in account and the shotgun stock is of Circassian

But muscle, nevertheless, he thought sadly. The works. Hubbard shoots the stock option out from one Jesse Mulaney. He shoots Mulaney's name off office door. This time it will be worse than usual because I do like that fat, fumbling, nervy, scared son-of-a-bitch—for reasons which escape me.

He collected his suitcase from the baggage pen and headed for a distant door which seemed as if it might lead to taxicabs. He hefted the suitcase and wondered if Jan had repacked it with the kind of clothing he would need. Though she had yet to fail him, he always felt unprepared when he did not have the time and opportunity to do his own packing. This time there had been even less notice than usual, and Jan had hustled the suitcase to the airport at almost the last moment, with even her good disposition showing signs of erosion.

He pulled the cab door shut and said, "The Sultana, please."

"Sultana coming up," the driver said and wrenched the cab away from the curb. They sped through the empty six o'clock streets on octagonal wheels with a continuous bounce, bang and rumble of springs and shocks. The interior stank of a harsh antiseptic vividly flavored with mint, a device which failed to accomplish its purpose, to conceal the illness of a passenger carried not very long ago. Hubbard rolled the nearest window down the rest of the way and lit a cigarette. The damp warm air blew in on him, coming from some endless cellar full of ripe mushrooms and old swimming trunks. On the causeway the air had a fresher, saltier scent. The street lights went out. An old man in what looked like bright yellow pajamas fled across the road in front of the cab and turned to shriek an obscenity. An ambulance sped past them with descending dopler scream, a prowl car close behind it. Above the entrance to a strip joint was a forty-foot-high plywood silhouette of someone named Saturday Jones. The beach street wore a compacted, sodden litter that looked as if parades had gone by, honoring the more ancient perversions.

The cab headed north past increasingly arrogant and fanciful hotel structures. A massive woman in white slacks and white halter strolled the lonely sidewalk with a small

...ng dog on a leash. Hubbard had to look back to ...ure himself that the dog was not pale purple, but it was. The static fronds of all the palm trees were obviously the product of patience, metal shears and an endless supply of green enameled tin. The bursting beds of flowers were vulgarities perpetrated by thousands of busy-fingered, stone-faced little Polish women.

The driver yanked the cab through a mausoleum gate and up a glossy acreage of asphalt. Before the cab plunged under the daring tilt of the cantilevered roof that sheltered the main entrance, Hubbard caught a glimpse of a huge black, white and red banner which said, "Welcome APETOD!!!"

The cab stopped with a dual complaint of tires and brakes, and the driver said with dreary pride, "Sultana, nineteenahalf minutes."

A big doorman with a meaty, military face came gravely to take the two pieces of luggage. Hubbard paid the driver. Three stout disheveled men were standing in a patch of ornamental shrubbery. They wore tropical suits, ragged straw peon hats and big round convention buttons.

"Goddam it, Hank," one of them was saying loudly. "Every goddam time we all agree *I'm* going to take the tenor, you come in and take it too. Now goddam it dyah wanna sing it right or dyah wanna sing it wrong?"

The plate-glass door swung shut, and Hubbard walked on thick carpeting in a chill that felt five degrees lower than the terminal building had been. As he walked toward the distant registration desk, he puzzled over APETOD. Association for the Prevention of? Of what? Everything Tough Or Dirty. Sign me up, brothers. I will join.

In remote corners and alcoves and setbacks of the lobby area, work gangs were sweeping, polishing, cleaning, rearranging. He looked at the complex vistas of ramps and glass, pastels and plastics, at all the contrived decadence of crypto-modern, and remembered that a friend of his had once described the decor of a neighboring hotel as being Early Dental Plate. The huge hotel, now being brushed and polished by the maintenance crews, was like some bawdy, obese, degenerate old queen who, having endured prolonged orgy, was now

being temporarily restored to a suitably regal
by all the knaves and wenches who serve her.

The desk clerk had a varnished wave in his baby
hair, and adorably narrow little lapels, and a bruised a.
winsome little mouth to smile with, and the eyes of one
of the larger lizards, unwinking, unforgiving.

"Mr. Hubbard?" he said. He caressed his Cardex. "Oh
dear," he said. "We have nothing reserved, no."

"Try American General Machine."

"Oh, yes!" the clerk cooed. "Yes indeed. Coming in today, with the convention. Lovely accommodations, sir.
Eighth floor, north wing, with an ocean suite and other
rooms. I have it all reserved under a Mr. Mulaney.
Would that be correct? A party of ten?"

"That would be correct."

"Would Mr. Mulaney be making the room assignments
for the group?"

"He'll be happy to have me pick my own. What's
reserved?"

The clerk drifted away and came back with a room
chart sealed in plastic. "This is a standard floor plan,
sir, for all our north wing floors, with the numbers the
same except, of course, the floor designation digit miss-
ing. Let me see now. You have the master suite at the
end, a three-bedroom suite and this smaller adjacent
suite and this pair of interconnecting singles and the three
singles along this side. Um, yes. That would be ten,
wouldn't it? Of course."

"Any of these three singles will be fine."

"But, sir, as long as you are the first one here, you
could be on the ocean side. These are really the less desirable . . ."

"It's what I'd like," Hubbard said, and hoped the clerk
wouldn't break into tears. "Can you give me one now?"

"Oh gracious, that might be a problem. APETOD had
their farewell banquet last night. We might have to move
you later in the day, give you some other . . . Let me
check with the housekeeper on eight north, sir."

The clerk murmured into a phone, hung up and smiled
in a sweet and happy way. "Eight forty-seven is available,
sir. We won't have to move you."

"Fine, fine," Hubbard said, and hoped the lad
wouldn't collapse with joy.

A soft chime summoned a bellhop who led Hubbard

proper bank of elevators. They walked a long way own the total silence of the eighth floor. A house-keeping cart stood outside the open door of 847. A brawny monochromatic woman in white was stripping the twin beds. She looked at them with total hostility.

"This was supposed to be ready," the bellhop said.

"So who says suppose? So who knows about ready? Do forty-seven she says, so I do it."

"So do it," the bellhop said.

"It's all right," Hubbard said. "It doesn't matter." He tipped the boy. The room smelled of stale cigar and a faint pungency of perfume. He took off his hat and jacket and loosened his tie. Sliding a glass door aside, he stepped out onto a tiny triangular terrace, just big enough for the chaise fashioned of aluminum and plastic webbing and one small metal table. The vertical sawtooth construction of the side of the building gave the terraces the illusion of privacy. A tall glass containing a collapsed straw, an inch of pale orange liquid and a poisonous-looking cherry stood on the railing. He leaned on the railing and looked down at orderly arrangements of acres of sun cots, at two pools, one Olympic and the other larger and freeform, at a thatched bar and a pagoda bar, at the empty alignment of outdoor tables and chairs, and the lush calligraphy of the planting areas. The sun was be-hind him, shining on tall pale distant buildings, leaving the area below him in blue-gray shadow.

The woman came out and snatched the glass, looked around for other debris, snorted and went back into the room. "Now it's done!" she bellowed a few minutes later. As he turned, the corridor door slammed shut.

He unpacked. Jan had done well. But there was no fond funny note, no silly present for him. Of course, he told himself, she had no time for such nonsense. Not this time. The room had the sterility of a place where no one had ever lived. The little stains and abrasions and scars had been cleverly added to make him believe he was not the last living man in the world. The machines did not want him to be too lonely, so they added these sub-liminal clues.

He ordered up juice, eggs, cocoa and a morning paper. After he finished, he pushed the cart out into the hall, closed the terrace door, pulled the draperies shut. He turned a bedlight on, showered, put on his pajamas, got into bed. By then it was late enough to place the call to Jan.

"Was it a good trip, dear?" she asked. Her voice was dimmed by the humming distance, flat and uninvolved.

"They tried to cut us off at the waterhole, but we fought our way out."

"What? I couldn't hear you, dear. Mike was bellering."

"It was okay. I got some sleep."

"Thats good. Mike wants to talk to you."

"Daddy! Daddy! You know what, Daddy! I'm *limping*!"

"Now how about that!"

"When you come home I'll be *limping*! Are you coming home now?"

"Pretty soon, boy." When Jan came back on the line he said, "What's with the limp?"

"It's very convincing, when he doesn't forget which leg it is. He turned his ankle and demanded a bandage. How's the weather there?"

"Tropical. By the way, I'm in eight forty-seven."

"Have a truly hilarious convention, dear."

"Thanks so much. This won't be a picnic. You know what I have to do."

Her voice was inaudible for a moment. ". . . not many picnics for anybody any more. I miss them. Thanks for calling. Keep in touch, dear."

"I will. I will indeed. Love you."

"Also, of course. Rest up, if they give you the chance. 'Bye."

After he hung up he had a premonition of what could happen. The district man, whichever one had been stuck with the mechanics of the arrangements for the AGM group, would be over to check everything out. And he would find Hubbard was already registered and in, and he would feel terribly anxious to make certain that Mr. Hubbard was ecstatically content with everything.

He picked up the phone again and said, "This is Floyd Hubbard in eight forty-seven. Put a no-call on this line, please, and take it off at noon."

He set his travel alarm for noon, turned out the bedlamp, and nestled himself into the whispering chill. The new womb for the new man, he thought. No sounds intrude. This chilled washed air is the same in Boston, Houston and Washoe. And darkness is standard issue everywhere. Here you are, Hubbard, with your invisible hatchet and the ineradicable mark of the assassin. This hurts me as much as it does you, Jesse. He burrowed his grateful way down into sleep.

Two

FRED FRICK, Assistant District Supervisor, arrived at the Sultana at ten A.M., accompanied by one of the road men, a mild round swarthy young man named Fayhouser. Frick was in his early forties, a lean sandy jittery man with pale restless blue eyes, a sharp, high-pitched voice, a rather ugly and feral mouth full of oversized yellowed teeth. He always gave the impression of being too sharply dressed, too dapper, yet taken item by item his clothing was always in good conservative taste. There was something about the shape of him and his manner which gave the casual observer the impression that his underwear, at least, had to be of lavender silk to match concealed sleeve garters.

They walked to the Sultana from a large parking lot a block and a half away. Frick stopped and looked at the big banner just being fastened in place. "Welcome to the Joint Convention of COLUDA and NAPATAN."

"Pair of belly dancers," Fayhouser said.

Frick turned and fixed Fayhouser with a cold glare. "Bobby, that kind of crap is okay between you and me because I know your attitude is generally good. But don't you start making any smart cracks in front of the wrong people."

"Sure, Fred," Fayhouser said uneasily.

"There's a lot of guys, and we work for some of them, take the National Association maybe a little more serious than they do their daughter's virginity, and you come out with any cute remarks, they mark you some kind of a Communist. This is your first convention, and about the whole thing, Bobby, your attitude is you got to be eager and reverent."

"All right, Fred. I didn't mean anything."

"Let's get some coffee and get organized."

They went into the hotel and down to the lower level,

past the shops of furs and jewels to the Persian Grill and sat in the swivel armchairs at the low counter.

Frick opened a small leather notebook and uncapped a gold pen.

"About the Hospitality Suite, Bobby, I am going to go over it one more time with you. I am in charge of *all* the arrangements for our team, and you are my deputy in charge of the suite. You know the other road men you're going to have to work with. You keep them in line. Every man comes into the AGM suite, he gets a drink in his hand fast. You and the other boys can drink, but keep them weak. A mild buzz is okay, but nothing more. You all keep smiling. You introduce everybody to everybody, and you do more listening than talking, and you laugh at the jokes."

"Eager and reverent," Fayhouser said.

Frick looked at him narrowly. "Exactly. Keep the opened bottles out and the full ones in a bedroom closet. Spread cigarettes around. Keep the ashtrays clean. What'll be a help, line up one bellhop and hit him pretty good to start, with a promise of more at the end if he takes care of you, which means checking all the time without being called to make sure we got ice and mix and so on. Do the same with a maid on eight, so she can come and hoe the place out whenever it isn't busy."

"Right!"

"You're getting a hell of a break, Bobby, because this way you get to meet AGM brass that wouldn't know you're alive otherwise. I'll be around a lot of the time, of course, but there can be special problems you got to watch. One is, of course, any of the boys we picked for this job getting out of line in any way. It could hurt me and it could hurt you. Once in Atlanta, at a NAPATAN regional convention, one of Federal's road men helping out in the suite goosed the wife of the executive vice-president down from New York. Federal cleaned out that whole regional organization."

"No goosing. Got ya!"

"Dammit, Bobby, if you're not going to take this seriously . . ."

"I'm taking it seriously, honest, Fred."

Frick sighed. "Okay. What I was saying, if one of our boys gets plotzed, we run him off the team fast before any damage is done. Another problem, the guy who has hit too many suites and is a drunk nuisance by the time he gets to ours. Check the badge. If he's brass, all you can do is handle it the best way you know how. Maybe he's a lousy road man from some other outfit. Then move him out, firm and fast. Send him along. Tell him they got broads at the Federal suite, or at United. Let the competition worry about him. Which brings up a new problem. Broads. I got a bedroom set aside for you boys working the suite, and there's no real need for more than two of us to be in the suite at the same time. If you get something lined up, okay. So long as you handle it with good taste. Don't bring broads into the suite. And don't let anybody get so carried away, he can't take his turn in the suite. This is a case of just using horse sense."

"I understand."

Frick studied his notebook intently for a few moments, then put it back in his pocket. "Now you go check when we can get the suite, and I'll go see how Tommy's coming with the exhibit."

The Sultana had been planned and constructed as a resort-convention hotel, and the huge convention hall was a separate structure, joined to it by an umbilical corridor eighty feet wide and over two hundred feet long. This corridor was adjacent to the Arabian Room, the main dining room of the hotel. When no convention was in progress, or when the convention hall was being used as a sports arena, the corridor could be blocked off by an intricate accordion-door system. When a convention was in progress, the corridor formed an ideal place for exhibits. The lighting, electric outlets, floor covering—had all been planned with this use in mind.

Most of the exhibits were up, and a hundred people were adding the finishing touches. Many of them had a look of total exhaustion. The deadline for removal of the APETOD exhibits had been ten o'clock the previous evening, and many of the people had worked straight through.

Fred Frick walked swiftly through the noises and confusions to the AGM exhibit. Tommy Carmer was opening cartons of color press literature and stacking them on a narrow table just inside the blue velvet rope. A pair of pretty twin blondes in tight plaid pants and sheer blouses watched him with a marked lack of interest. A man in coveralls was sitting on the floor working on a small electric motor. Carmer was a sallow man with a hollow chest, a great naked dome of forehead, and very little chin.

"How's it look to you, Freddy?"

"Goddam, it looks great! For once we don't get stuck over in a corner someplace. What's he doing?"

"Oh, that's the motor that makes the parts move in the big cutaway display. It quit a minute after I turned it on."

"Can he fix it?"

"He says so."

Frick turned toward the blondes. "How are you today, girls? Ready to go?"

One shrugged. The other one said listlessly, "Any time." They had show girl figures rather than model figures. They looked sulky and bored.

"Which is Honey and which is Bunny?" Frick asked.

"I'm Honey, with the mole," one of them said, and touched her cheek.

"You going to dog it, girls, or you going to give it the pazzazz?"

"You'll get what you're paying for," Bunny said. "You got any beef, you call the agency, okay?"

"Let's hear the spiel, girls."

They shrugged simultaneously, moved into position. The sudden change in them was electrifying. They became alert, vivacious, with sparkling eyes, big media smiles, arched backs and thrust breasts. They took the alternate lines of the demonstration talk they had learned, and came in on the punch line in unison. Then they immediately lapsed back into sullen boredom.

"That's great!" Frick cried. "It's exciting!"

"You pay for pros, you get pros," Bunny said.

"They all clear on the questions and answers, Tommy?" Frick asked.

"Check them if you want."

He asked them the questions usually asked about AGM products and installations, and got the right answers. He threw them one he knew was beyond them, and got the proper referral to "our Mr. Carmer."

"Yeah, Tommy, this ties in perfect with the promotion. Girls, you know the hours you're going to work. You take your orders from Tommy. And I don't want you spelling each other. You're either both here or both gone. One of you has to go to the can, you both go. No drinking, and no dating the guys that'll sure as hell make a try."

"Any time we can't brush off a bunch of crummy convention . . ."

"Okay. Now what'll you wear? I want to see plenty of bazoom, kids."

"You'll see more than you can handle, pops," Honey said.

"That's all set," Tommy said.

"And don't you kids be standing around like you are right now, looking like you hated the whole deal."

"When we're on, we'll be on, friend," Bunny said. "You'll have no complaint."

Bobby Fayhouser came up behind Frick and said, "Fred, can I see you a minute?"

"You girls be back here at two o'clock sharp, ready to go," Frick said. They nodded and walked away, side by side, in perfect unison. Frick watched the synchronous clench and roll and swing of the plaid fannies and shook his head wonderingly and said, "Like seeing double, huh? Tommy, maybe there's our little celebration when this damn thing is over."

"I doubt the hell out of that," Carmer said. "That Honey one has a two-year-old kid and is married to a musician, and the other one has a county cop for a boyfriend. That'll be okay on this job, Freddy, but the reason they're a little sour, it's on account of they've been singing and dancing since they were three years old, and now they're twenty-three, and I guess they think they should have made it a little better than being in a convention display."

"It might be important, what I want to tell you, Fred," Fayhouser said.

Frick moved off to one side with the younger man. "A delay on the suite?" he asked.

"You were worried about a man named Hubbard coming? Floyd Hubbard? And you asked me to tell you right away if . . ."

"Is he coming?"

"He's already here. He's in 847. He checked in before seven o'clock this morning."

Frick looked beyond Fayhouser, looked toward the huge shadowy cave of the convention hall beyond the display ramp, and exposed his unlikely teeth in a mirthless grin. "Well, well, well! So he made it."

"What's the bit on him anyhow, Fred? I know you put him on the AGM list, but you seemed nervous about him. Is there anything I should know?"

Frick stared at Fayhouser with an odd indignant contempt. "You? What should you know about him? He's home-office brass, isn't he? So you treat him like home-office brass. What does a kid like you have to worry about? They test all of you these days, don't they? Your marks are on file in some goddam computer, aren't they? You got papers like a pedigree dog."

"But . . ."

"Don't stand too close to this Hubbard, or you'll hear all the little relays clicking and it might make you nervous."

"Why get sore at me?"

"I'm not sore at you, Bobby. When do we get the suite?"

"Noon at the latest."

"So go do something useful."

Bobby Fayhouser walked away. He glanced back once and then quickened his pace. Frick walked slowly toward the main lobby, glancing at the exhibits. He phoned 847 from the lobby and was told there was no answer—which could mean that Hubbard was out or was blocking all incoming calls.

It was eleven o'clock, too late to get in touch with Jesse Mulaney and tip him off about Hubbard. Maybe Jesse knew it anyway. But, as the local representative, the man on the scene, it was his job to keep Mulaney advised. A rich territory, but he wished to God this convention was somewhere else this time, not in his back yard. Poor Jesse, too old-time for the new hot shots.

He walked out a side door and down an outside staircase to the pool area. The sun blazed down on the ranked battalions of sun cots, more than half of them occupied. By the cabanas the people who paid the fee for more privacy were sunning themselves. He walked to the thatched bar, sat on a shady stool, ordered a Screwdriver and felt his morale improve as he watched the bartender slice the fresh oranges. After his first deep swallow of the drink, he looked through an opening of the bamboo framework around the bar and watched a hard-faced blonde with a lithe youthful body oil herself with most tender care, then stretch out and become another anonymous sun-stricken corpse amid the acres of browning, gleaming flesh.

Jesse, he decided, would have some operational plan. He wouldn't tattoo a dotted line on his throat and then kneel down to make it handier for this Hubbard. Where it puts me, he thought, is right the hell in the middle. I ride with Mulaney, and I go out when he does, which could be a soon thing. If I should back off from it and Mulaney wins, then he would delight in throwing me out, because he would notice that kind of thing sooner than any man I've ever known. Mulaney will at least get pensioned. What the hell will I get?

Suddenly he thought of one safe move he could make, one that might look good to Mulaney, and wouldn't be known to anyone else. Hell, he thought, Jesse might go for it and it might work, even. He finished his drink in a hurry and went into the hotel, to the pay booths on the lower level. He looked up an unlisted number in the back of his pocket notebook.

After the sixth ring, just as he was beginning to wonder if she was out of town, a woman answered, her voice sulky and blurred with sleep, asking an angry question which came out sounding like, "Wharrawah?"

"Alma? Alma, honey? This is Freddy. Freddy Frick."

"Oh dear Jesus! 'S dawn, Freddy! Cold, gray dawn."

"Alma, the reason I called . . ."

"Hol' the phone a minute."

He held the phone a long long time. "Now what?" she asked, and her voice was clear and almost precise.

"Jesse is coming down. To a convention. He'll get here today."

"This is a reason to wake me up, for God's sake? He's a dear man, and we've had our laughs, Freddy, but sleep is important."

"Alma, I always had the feeling you liked Jesse Mulaney."

"I guess I do."

"More than just . . . on a business basis."

"What the hell are you getting at?"

"Alma, maybe he's in trouble. He didn't ask me to get in touch with you. It's my idea entirely. I was just thinking . . . maybe you could help."

"Keep talking."

"There's a lot of changes going on, in the company.

There's a man going to be at the convention, and he will maybe be making the final report that'll tie the can to Jesse. I was just thinking that . . . if this man had a hell of a good time down here, and if it got to be . . . well, say a little bit obvious toward the end, he wouldn't be so anxious to take the wrong kind of word back."

"It isn't exactly a new problem, Freddy dear. I suppose this man would have his guard up. I mean to say that if he's bright, which I suppose he would have to be, he might be expecting this sort of thing, and so it wouldn't work."

"There's that chance, Alma. So it would depend on the talent, I guess."

"It would indeed. It would indeed."

"On the other hand, maybe Jesse has a better plan worked out, and wouldn't want to try anything like this. But I figured it wouldn't do any harm to check it out before he gets here, so it could be lined up in case."

"This man you want should have a fine time—young?"

"Early thirties."

"That makes it a little rougher you know. Married?"

"Yes."

"That's a small help, usually. There would have to be some good reason for having the girl there, you know. Have you thought of that?"

"Yes, as we've been talking I've thought of it, but it would have to be a cover story that would fit the girl, Alma."

"You know, you're always just a little sharper than I expect you to be, Freddy."

"Should I say thanks?"

"While we've been talking, dear, I've been weeding out. I have a very lovely little friend who might work out just right. But it would depend on how she takes to it. She's kind of complicated. She's certainly not what you'd call obvious. Sometimes she's more trouble than she's worth. Now don't get nervous, dear. I don't mean she gets taken drunk or neurotic. I mean she's too damn selective sometimes. And stubborn as can be. But let me put it this way, Freddy. For any truly high-level guy wanting to meet a nice little friend, I'd have every confidence in Cory. Her name, dear, is Corinna. But then, how many high-level guys are ever in need?"

"Jesse is in need."

"In another way, of course. But when can you let me know for sure?"

"Before four o'clock this afternoon. Will that be okay?"

"That will be fine, Freddy dear. But this business about a favor for dear old Jesse has nothing to do with . . . your little token of gratitude for setting it up."

"You know I wouldn't try to short you, Alma."

"I think you might try, but it wouldn't work. I should warn you, dear, the whole thing might work out a little high."

"A lot of little things can get buried in a convention tab."

"If you tell me it's a deal, we'll set it up over the phone where Cory should meet you for the briefing. Okay?"

"That would seem to do it, Alma. I'm sorry I woke you up."

"I'm glad you did, really. You know, I ought to feel a little angry with you, Freddy. I haven't heard from you in ever so long. Way last Christmas, wasn't it?"

"Yes. I remember. It's this way, Alma. There was this merger, over a year ago, and things have got pretty tightened up. They put in these damn control systems, and it clamps down on me, so I don't get the chance to operate like in the old days. I mean it would have to come out of my pocket, and that sort of slows me down. Even that deal last Christmas, I could only swindle half the tab, so it was a calculated risk."

"But weren't they darling girls?"

"They sure were."

"Weren't the men some kind of politicians?"

"A special purchasing commission from Alabama. The deal was to get the low bid thrown out so we'd be the ones to get it."

"And you did?"

"Sure enough, Alma. So I got the rest of the fee back out of my override, and it worked out. But I don't think it's ever going to get back to the way it was back in the good old days when Jesse was down here in my job and I was working for him."

"It's the way everybody is cracking down on expense accounts, Freddy, and believe me, it's put the bind on my business. I'm down to about a third, honestly. Those *were* the good old days, I guess. Remember when Jesse

had that special sign made up for me? For my desk?
Technical Consultant—Sales Staff—American General
Machine—Southeast District. I've still got it around here
someplace. You know, aside from the laughs, I'm awful
damn grateful to Jesse on another count. In fifty-one,
it was, he started me in buying AGM. Before that all
I ever bought was government bonds. For three years
I bought AGM, and then it started to look as if I had
holes in my head. Honest to God, Freddy, two years ago
it dropped like a rocket. I called Jesse long distance
about it a half dozen times. Did you know that?"

"No, I didn't."

"He kept telling me to hang on, and thank God I
did. That merger thing made me fat. I got three shares
of GAE for every two of AGM, and you know where
the hell that has gone to in the last year."

"I know, I know. Speaking of GAE, that's where this
Hubbard came over from, the one maybe Cory will get
to meet. Actually now we're the AGM division of
GAE, Inc."

"Anyhow, tell Jesse I'm grateful. Give him my new
number, Freddy dear, and tell him to give me a ring
while he's in town. Maybe he could come over here for
a drink. Will Connie be with him?"

"Yes, I'm afraid so."

"Where is this deal?"

"The Sultana."

"So it's a ten-minute cab ride. He could slip out. How
are things with you, Freddy? How's Bert?"

"Well, not so good. It's a change of life thing, I guess,
but she doesn't want to admit it. She's always been a
nervous woman anyhow. Anyway, the kids are doing good.
Kit's getting good marks in Gainsville, and the Marines
just sent Tommy to a special school, some kind of radar
thing."

"You get Bert onto some hormones, Freddy, and you'll
see one hell of a change in her."

"There better be a change before she drives me nuts."

"I'll tell you what I'll do. I'll give Cory a special
briefing on this and tell her that it means a lot to me
personally if she does a good job."

"I'd appreciate that a lot, Alma."

"She's got a college degree."

"That could be a help in a deal like this. There's more

than just Jesse involved. He was the one hired me. We've
been close ever since. Maybe I've done a little too much
bitching about all the contol systems they've stuck in.
I guess I wouldn't have done so much bitching if I'd
realized they might get rid of Jesse."

"Why would they want to?"

"Maybe he's too old timey, Alma. Hell, I don't know.
He could sell sun glasses in a coal mine, but he couldn't
write up a ten-page analysis of how anybody else should
go about it, and he doesn't know a market survey from a
bagel."

"Isn't a convention a crazy place to come to to fire
a man?"

"They don't do it that way. He wouldn't be fired here.
We got tipped off they'd been evaluating him in every
other aspect of his job, and this is the last part of it
left, how he handles himself in this kind of a deal, how
much good he does AGM. Hubbard is one of the guys
they got doing those evaluations. They're a cold-fish
operation. They've weeded out the other divisions, and
now they've got around to sales, promotion and advertising. What they don't understand, there was never anything wrong with AGM sales. When we slipped, it was
on account of they fell behind on the design and research, so the other outfits had better products on the
market. We're damn near caught up already."

"Somebody at the door, dear. You phone me a yes
or no, okay?"

"Okay, Alma. And thanks a lot."

He hung up and went up into the main lobby. The convention registration desk had been set up. COLUDA and
NAPATAN delegates had begun to arrive. Their baggage
had begun to clutter the lobby, awaiting the rooms
being vacated by the delegates of the convention which
had just terminated. The cashiers were busy checking
out the APETOD people. There was a worn, weary, rueful
flavor about the APETOD people checking out which was
in sharp contrast with the holiday anticipation of the
groups of men who stood near the convention registration
tables. Fred Frick, moving toward the table, had to stop
a half dozen times to shake hands with friends employed
by other outfits in the industry, most of whom he hadn't
seen since the last regional convention.

He went to the NAPATAN table where a rather briskly

officious young lady said, "Welcome to the seventeenth annual convention of NAPATAN, Mr. . . . ?"

"Frick. Fred Frick, American General Machine."

She quickly extracted a card from her index. A slip of cardboard was stapled to the card. She tore it off at the perforation, deftly inserted it behind the transparent plastic of a lapel button. "Here, sir, is your badge. This is your convention program. This is your book of tickets which should be presented at all lunches, dinners and official cocktail parties. You will find one ticket for each event in your book." She looked at the card again. "There are fourteen in your group?"

"Yes. Ten in the hotel and four local."

"I see the whole group is prepaid, sir, except for the registration fee itself. That will be ten dollars. Do you wish to pick up the badges and programs and booklets for your entire group right now?"

"Thanks. I'll have someone else do that a little later, Miss. Uh . . . on second thought, I'll get the things for Mr. Hubbard now. Floyd Hubbard."

He paid her twenty dollars and walked diagonally across the lobby to the hotel registration desk. There he acquired an envelope. He put Hubbard's materials in the envelope, hesitated, then scrawled across the front of it, "Welcome aboard!!!! Fred Frick." He had the envelope placed in the rack for 847.

He moved along to the next section of the registration desk.

"Yes sir?"

"You have a reservation for me? John Dempsey."

"Ummmm . . . yes, Mr. Dempsey. A single. Are you with the convention?"

"No," Frick said, filling out the registration card.

"How long will you be with us?"

"I'll leave next Sunday."

"We can offer you a choice of . . ."

"Put me as far from the convention accommodations as you can get me. A nice room, please, but I don't have to stare at the ocean."

"Ummmm . . . eleven-oh-two is a nice room, Mr. Dempsey, in the main part of the structure here on the street side. Your luggage is here?"

"It'll be along later."

"Is this a charge, sir?"

"Cash. Do you want any right now?"

After a slight hesitation, appraisal, decision, the clerk smiled and said, "That won't be necessary, sir. I hope you'll enjoy your stay with us. Shall I have a boy show you . . ."

"Not right now, thanks," Frick said and pocketed his key and walked away from the desk. It was standard procedure devised a long time ago by Frick and Jesse Mulaney, and they had picked a name easy to remember even when drunk. The most predictable aspect of any convention was the certainty that the unpredictable problem would arise. And the availability of an anonymous room far from the turmoil of convention was a handy device. When checkout time came, the room could be billed right along with the rest of the AGM tab.

He went up to 1102 and found it a pleasant, sizable twin-bed room. It was a few minutes after twelve. He phoned the AGM suite, and Bobby Fayhouser answered.

"How are you doing, Bobby?"

"Okay, I guess. I raised some hell, and they're yanking a big rug out of here and replacing it. Near as I can figure, somebody built a camp fire in the middle of the main room here and put it out with catsup. I had three assistant managers up here clucking about it. Otherwise the place is okay."

"How about that little diarama display?"

"It's on the way over."

"Who have you got there with you?"

"Charlie and Les."

"When can I come make an inspection?"

"We should be all set by one o'clock anyway, Fred."

"Better than I expected. Look, I checked myself in at the convention desk, and I picked up Hubbard's stuff too. That check you got made out to NAPATAN is for a hundred 'n forty, right? Okay, first chance you get, go down and pick up the crap for the whole group and get twenty cash out of her, which you'll owe me. If she makes a fuss, tell me. She looks like a little doll who enjoys fussing. One thing I forgot to tell you. Scrounge all the glasses you can. I'll be around later on."

Next he called his home. Bert said, "This is a real considerate time to tell me whether or not you're coming home for lunch."

"Honey, I told you I can't be home for lunch *or* dinner, not while the convention is going on."

"You may think you told me but you didn't."

"Honestly, honey, I don't like this any better than you do, but I swear I don't have any idea when I'll be able to get home tonight."

"Oh, I knew so damn well that if that Jesse Mulaney came down, I wouldn't see you at all."

"Now baby . . ."

"Don't give me that now baby stuff, Frederick. It doesn't do any good. I don't know what you're up to, but I know you're damn glad to get away from me. You couldn't wait to get out of the house this morning, could you?"

"Honey, I've got a lot of responsibilities here. I got to see that the AGM part of this thing runs smooth, or that brass that comes down is going to think Fred Frick is a bum."

"The cat has been throwing up again."

"I'm sorry to hear that, honey."

"I've been cleaning up after him all morning."

"That's a shame."

"If you ever happen to think of it, and you're not too drunk, call me up again some time and say hello." She hung up so strenuously the noise made him flinch.

He tried 847 again. He was so convinced there would be no answer that when Hubbard said, "Hello?" it caught him off balance.

"Oh . . . uh . . . Mr. Hubbard? This is Fred Frick. We've never met, but . . ."

"Mr. Frick. Of course."

"Glad you could make it. I guess you got in real early."

"Earlier than I wanted to. But all they could do for me on anything later was put me on standby. So I decided at the last minute to play it safe and take a night coach."

"Is your room okay?"

"Fine. Fine."

"What I did, I signed you in for the convention and left the badge and stuff at the desk for you. I can phone down and have them shoot it right up to . . ."

"Thanks. I'll pick it up when I go down there."

"As you probably know already, Mr. Hubbard, this thing doesn't officially get off the ground until the opening banquet tonight in the Arabian Room at eight o'clock. I'd like to ask you to have lunch with me, but I've got to go out to the airport to meet Jesse and Mrs. Mulaney. Would you want to go out there with me?"

"I guess I'll wait until they get settled in. I think that would be better."

"Anything you say. What I was thinking, some of my boys are getting the AGM hospitality suite in shape, and if you're not doing anything else, I could stop by in say five minutes and take you down to the suite and introduce you to some of the boys, and we could have a little drink maybe."

"That's very kind of you, Mr. Frick. Five minutes?"

"Right."

Frick called the suite. Bobby wasn't there. Les Lewis said he was due back any minute and, yes, the suite was shaping up, and they could fix a drink. Frick explained the situation.

When he rapped at the door of 847, Hubbard opened it immediately, smiled, shook hands, came out into the hall and checked the door to be sure it had locked. Fred Frick felt slightly off balance. Hubbard was not the type he had anticipated. He was a stocky man, with considerable breadth of shoulder, and a look of toughness of body, of a resilient fitness. His black hair was cropped to a length which left just enough to comb and part. His lightweight suit, though obviously tailored to fit him very well, looked as if it was not the sort of thing he would ordinarily wear. He had big hands, a hard thrust of jaw, black and bushy brows, a nose slightly misshapen from some old breakage, a friendly grin, warm, brown, direct eyes. He gave Frick an impression of uncomplicated honesty. Frick knew the type. This man was some kind of technician. He would be more comfortable in coveralls. The hatchet men were cooler types, reserved, watchful, chronically skeptical.

As they walked toward the suite, Frick said, "Have you been to many of this sort of convention, Mr. Hubbard?"

"I've been to conventions, but not this kind. I guess they're all alike in a lot of ways. Mine were engineering deals."

Frick was gratified to have hit it so closely. "Oh, you started on the production side?"

Hubbard stopped outside the open door of the suite.

"Not production as such, Mr. Frick. Once upon a time I was a metallurgist. It wasn't so long ago, but it's beginning to seem like a long time ago. GAE hired me away from a research and testing lab to head up a research program on high conductivity metals, and it turned out bigger than they thought, so I had to get more and more over onto the administration side. Much to my disgust, Mr. Frick, they think I'm a better administrator than a metallurgist. So I'm stuck with it for a while. And they keep exposing me to every facet of the whole deal." He grinned, and Frick found it infectious "They keep me in a constant condition of confusion."

"Me, I've been in sales all my life," Frick said.

"Yes," Floyd Hubbard said. "I know."

In that moment of exposure Frick tried to make a reading, and got no further than Hubbard's brown friendly eyes. A metallurgist, Frick thought, and one hell of a man at a table stakes game.

"Come on in and meet the boys," Frick said.

Three

AT five minutes of three the Mulaneys were at last alone in their room in the Sultana. Jesse had checked the first room and decided it was too close to the rest of the AGM group, and Fred Frick had arranged a swap which gave them 832, a bedroom-sitting-room layout on the ocean side. Connie Mulaney was a trim, slim, handsome woman of fifty. Her hair was crisp and white, smartly coifed. Her bones were good, and her eyes were beautiful.

She hummed to herself as she performed the familiar routines of unpacking. Until the last few months, these past several years had been the happiest years of her life. After a pudgy girlhood and the nondescript years of motherhood, it seemed like a startling award for past meritorious behavior to suddenly come into one's own in the middle forties, into a strange resurgence of youthfulness when you had an awareness of how rare and valuable it was. It had given her a confidence she had never had before, and out of her confidence she had been able to give of herself and become treasured by many people. She knew the styles which suited her. She knew the mercilessness of time and fortune. And so she lived her days to the fullest and took splendid care of herself without permitting it to become obsessive.

As she transferred a stack of Jesse's white shirts to a bureau drawer, she looked at him in the mirror and stopped humming. He had stripped to his blue and white striped underwear shorts, and he sat on a bed staring out toward the ocean. Though she had never told him, and never would, when he was in repose he reminded her of a sad, tired clown resting after taking off his clown suit and his make-up. A big clown—the one who tags humbly along and keeps getting hit over the head with a bladder. He was a big man, overweight and flabby,

with skin as white as milk, a heavy pouch of belly, yet
with a bigness of frame and a solidity of back and
shoulders to remind her of the hard and husky man he
had been.

It was no longer possible to tell that his hair had
once been red. But he had the fair complexion of the
redhead, eroded and betrayed by the lifetime of rich
foods, expansive drinking, and all the late late nights.
His broad face was a pattern of small pouches, florid
with small broken veins. And out of this corroded monu-
ment to the gregariousness of man shone the light-blue
eyes, bland and young as those of any child.

She sighed inaudibly and finished the unpacking, and
hung her travel dress away. She walked around to
face him and said, "Now does it have to make you so
dreary to have brought me along, Jesse?"

He looked at her in quick protest. "No, honey! Hell,
I *want* you to come along with me. Every time."

She sat on the arm of a chair. "Now listen to the man.
All his life he's been saying that, but lately I really think
you've meant it, darling."

"I've always meant it."

"But if I'd always gone along, dear, think of all the
pleasure you'd have never been able to give all those
little girls at all the conventions and all the regional sales
conferences."

He showed by the sudden grin that he now realized
she had been needling him. "Truly thousands of them,
honey. Only a truly selfish man would have denied them
the special joys of Mulaney."

"Lecher!"

"Needler!"

She reached over and patted his knee and leaned back
again, feeling a little familiar twist in her heart as she
realized how much she loved this man. There had
been the women. She was almost dead certain of that, but
it was the *almost* which was the important word. And
there might be others yet, but never flaunted, never ad-
mitted, never permitted to shame her in any public or
secret way.

After a little time of silence she said, continuing an
argument which had gone on in oblique ways for three
months, "Couldn't you maybe have had enough of all of
it, dear? Couldn't you, without wanting to admit it to

yourself, be full up to here with all the . . all the pressure and the quotas and all the nasty little Fred Fricks."

"Nothing wrong with Freddy."

"So I shouldn't have said his name, but what about the rest of it?"

"The rest of what?"

"Please, darling. You know what I mean."

"Hell, I've been under pressure all my life."

"Not this kind, Jesse."

"I've fought to keep my job fifty times and you know it."

She moved over to sit on the bed beside him, and took his hand, lifted it to her cheek. "But before, darling, you always knew what you were fighting, and how to fight it. This time, you don't know what they want, really. Maybe all they want is change, for the sake of change. And you can't win if that's what they're after."

"They can't do this to me!"

"Darling, please."

"I know ten thousand men all over this country, Connie. I've hired them and fired them. Some of them I've either outsmarted or outsold. Goddam it, woman, what will all those boys be saying and thinking if Jesse Mulaney gets thrown out on his ear two whole years before the first retirement option? Don't you think I've got any pride?"

"I know you've got pride, Jesse. Too much, maybe. But what I mean is . . . is it really worth it? We've had good luck with the children. The retirement thing would be *almost* as much. And with the shrewd way you've bought stocks, dear, we don't even need the executive pension. Can't it be done in some way that would . . . save that pride of yours? A resignation for reasons of health?"

He slapped his chest. *"I'd* know I'd been whipped. And by what? Stupid forms, reports, evaluations, surveys. I'm being gutted by twerps. Crappy little slide-rule twerps, like Lansing and DeVrees and Hubbard."

"Floyd Hubbard seems quite nice, really."

He looked at her in a woebegone way. "Goddam it, Connie, I think of the ones they've pushed out in the past year. Ed, Chris, Wally. You know how it makes me feel? Like I was some big old extinct animal being chased through the swamps by a bunch of yapping dogs."

She smiled at him. "But you won't quit, will you?"

"I can't."

"Okay, Mr. Mulaney. I guess I'll just have to accept that, and stop boring from within, weakening the structure. They'll know they've been in a scrap. Okay?"

"Okay. I'm glad you're along this time especially, Connie. They expect me to mess something up. Maybe I would have, if I was alone. Lots of times I've looked bad, and didn't mean to, but it didn't matter. This time it does. You . . . you sort of keep an eye on me."

"Of course, darling. You don't need it, but I will."

She went to the other side of the room, took off her slip, bra and girdle, and put on a pale yellow robe. "What time do we have to be anywhere?"

"We ought to get to the suite about six o'clock."

"Are you going to have a nap, Jesse?"

"I guess so."

"Shower when you wake up?"

"Uh huh."

"I'll take mine now, I guess."

"Go ahead."

She stood at the bathroom door for a moment, looking at his broad white back. He sat with his shoulders slumped. She ran the back of her hand down the firmness of her hip and thigh. When this special attractiveness had come to her, late and unexpected, she had been delighted not only for her own sake, but for Jesse's as well. It seemed such a special boon, a glory of late afternoon on what had been not a very pretty day. A special favor to the man who had chosen her when she had begun to wonder if anybody ever would.

She dropped her toilet articles on her bed and went around and stood close in front of him. "You're all tensed up, darling," she said.

"A little bit."

She put her hands on his shoulders. "I'm the best of all possible sleeping pills, you know. No barbituate hangover."

"I knew I'd run into a girl at this convention," he said, and his voice had already changed in the husky way she knew.

She dropped the robe into the chair, and stretched out beside him on the bed, welcoming his arms, and all the familiarities of the sustaining, readying hands. This is where the meaning is, she thought. The final meaning, always so good that even when this too is gone, we'll live the time left in the glow of it. Thousands of times of love with this man, so that we are a single creature. And no other man has known me.

"Want to share?" he said huskily.

"Not close enough, darling. Next time around. Make it all for you."

So, reading the small clues rightly, she went astride him and took the guided depth of connection, and became lovingly industrious while he stroked the long lines of her back, until he surged under her, and gave a choking gasp, stilled the tumult of her hips with the strength of his hands, and gave a long dwindling sigh. She put her head on his chest and listened to the slowing canter of his heart.

"Getting better girls at these things all the time," he said sleepily.

"We're carefully screened," she said.

"Love you, Con."

"And I love you, Jesse Mulaney."

When she came out of her shower he was snoring just loud enough so she could hear him over the endless exhalation of the airconditioning grill. She put a blanket over him. She called the desk from the phone in the small sitting room and left a call for five fifteen.

She turned her bed down and got in and looked over at him.

It isn't fair, she thought. It just isn't the least bit fair. Thirty-two years with them, almost. Maybe, if I get the right chance, I can talk to Floyd Hubbard. I don't think he's like the others. He might be. That look of warmth and honesty might mean nothing at all. That would make him worse than the others. I think he ought to know what it will do to Jesse.

I wonder what Freddy Frick was being so darned conspiratorial about, taking Jesse off in a corner like that before we even got our luggage off the flight? Freddy is a shifty little bastard. When they came back to me, Jesse had that look he gets. Whenever he's guilty he looks right at me and makes his eyes rounder, and he speaks more carefully.

A few moments later she was asleep.

At a few minutes after five the phone rang in 1102, and Fred Frick stopped his pacing and grabbed it

"Mr. Frick? This is Miss Barlund. I'm in the lobby."

"Oh! Come right on up, please. Eleven-oh-two Can I order a drink for you while you're on your way up?"

"Yes, thank you. Scotch and water, tall, please"

After he placed the drink order, he opened the door a few inches and resumed his pacing. He had been almost positive Jesse would veto the idea. But he'd had to go through the motions with Alma, to be covered in case Jesse and Alma got together this trip. But Jesse had thought it over and said, "Why not? No matter what happens to me, I'd like to catch one of those little bastards acting human just one time."

"It could be a good piece of money, Jesse."

"Now are you trying to talk me out of it?"

"No. Nothing like that. But Hubbard shouldn't find out about it."

"Are you going to tell him? Am I? And Alma wouldn't send over anybody who'd pull anything cute. As far as the money goes, I'm not about to pinch a penny on a thing like this. If Alma says she's good, that's enough. How is Alma?"

"Same as ever. She's telling the girl she has a personal interest in this working out. And she'd like you to phone her. I've got her new number. She wants to thank you for the way the stock thing worked out."

"Go ahead with it, Freddy. Set it up. You make an outlay, you'll get it back. But Hubbard isn't going to be easy."

So now he was in it, and nervous about it, convinced it was a mistake before it had even begun.

At the knock on his door he hurried to it and opened it and got his first look at Corinna Barlund. Though he maintained the smile on his salesman face, he felt acute disappointment. She was of medium height, and to Frick she looked more scrawny than willowy. Her hair was more nearly brown than blonde, soft, cropped, casual, with a careful-careless arrangement of bangs. She wore a blue sheath dress, a little white cape effect, blue high-heeled sandals, white gloves, smoked glasses, and a Jacqueline pillbox hat. She carried one of the largest handbags Frick had ever seen.

"Mr. Frick," she said gravely.

"Nice you could make it, Cory," he said as she walked in.

"Thank you."

He stared at the rearview of her as he closed the door. She certainly walked in a pleasant, classy way, but who goes for the walk? Most teenagers had her whipped in front, and all she had in back was tan skinny legs and about as much can on her as any eleven-year-old boy.

"Sit down, Cory. Sit down. Drinks will be right along." She turned and smiled and lifted the big handbag. "I didn't know the uniform of the day, so I brought a change along, dinner dress and goodies to go with it." She turned the straight chair away from the desk, sat down and put the bag on the floor beside her. She put her dark glasses on the desk, shrugged her cape off her shoulders onto the back of the chair, and pulled her gloves off. She bent and delved in the big bag and came up with cigarettes. Frick hurried to light her cigarette. He sat on the bed and smiled at her and said, "Well, now!" Her bare shoulders were nicely tanned, but they looked too bony to him.

There was a second rap on the door. A waiter brought the two drinks in. He seemed far more polite and attentive than waiters usually were, Frick realized, when they brought you and a broad a drink. She had style, certainly. And what he classified as a society manner. This was the kind of bitch you'd see playing tennis when you looked over the wall into one of the private clubs. He suddenly decided she was maybe some society housewife Alma had lined up, a bored doll short of money and looking for kicks.

She sipped her drink. He smiled at her. He wondered what the most graceful way to bring up the problem.

"You *do* have the money, Mr. Frick?"

"Uh? Oh, yes. Yes, I got it right here." He took the envelope out of his inside pocket and took it over to her and went back to sit on the bed.

She counted it and put it in her purse. "And you do understand the way it's set up?"

"Alma said you'd make up your own mind, as you always do, and if you say no dice, you give me the money back, except for a hundred bucks."

"Fifty for me and fifty for Alma. But she'll try to find

somebody else for you, of course. As I understand it, an old friend of yours and Alma's will be helped out if a certain youngish married man makes a fool of himself at this convention. I'll have to meet him and have a chance to talk to him a little bit before I tell you if I'll take it on. I have an instinct for these relationships, Mr. Frick. And I can make a very good guess—which will keep you from wasting your money. Now tell me about this man."

"His name is Floyd Hubbard, and lately he's been working out of the Houston office. His wife is named Janice, and he's got a little boy four years old and a little girl not a year old yet. He gets good money, and he's a metallurgist by trade, on the research end."

"Describe him."

Frick did, to the best of his ability. As he had been talking, he had been looking at her. He had the strange feeling he could not bring her face into the proper focus. When he looked at the flat planes of her cheeks, he could not see the rest of her face. When he looked at her eyes, dark and gray-blue, the rest of her seemed blotted out somehow. Feature by feature, from the lean little nose to long firm heavy lips, to the small round imperative chin, everything seemed just right, except he could not see it all at once, as a face.

As he re-examined the rest of her, he had the feeling she'd acquired more curves and more ripeness since she'd walked in. He thought it strange that there seemed to be just exactly enough of everything. And everything had begun to look curiously precious, as if this woman had been fashioned with more than ordinary care. Suddenly he saw all of her at once, saw her face as a face, an entity, and saw that she was so lovely, he felt as if his heart had been slit and drained and hung empty in his chest. His hands began to sweat. To restore perspective, he began to examine her bare shoulders again and discovered that he could see no ugliness of bone, only a tenderness of hollows which demanded the gratitude of many kissings.

And it's all for sale, he thought. It was an incredible thought, one that threatened to blow a ragged hole in his brain tissue.

"That's all you can tell me about him?"

"That's all I know. Cory . . . uh . . . how did you . . . uh . . ."

She gave him a cold sweet smile. "How did a girl like me get into a life like this? Just lucky, I guess. Let's not waste time with that sort of nonsense, Mr. Frick. We have to come up with a plausible way for me to be thrown in contact with Floyd Hubbard, some way that won't make him suspicious. Any suggestions?"

"I haven't been able to come up with one. I mean we could say you're working for me, but it would look funny, I think."

"It would look implausible. I have one contact I could use that might work out. And it's actually a kind of work I tried to make a living at, approximately ten thousand years ago."

"Huh?"

"A friend of mine publishes a regional magazine, Mr. Frick. I even sold him some junk articles a long time ago." She looked at a tiny gold watch. "It's too late to phone him now. Conventions are a big local industry. I know I could sell him on the idea of my doing an article on one particular company at one particular convention. What's your company?"

"AGM. American General Machine."

"If I go ahead with it, my friend can clear me with the hotel PR man, and then anyone who happens to check will find out it is all true, true, true."

"So how come you pick this convention and pick us?"

"This convention fits into my busy schedule, let us say, Mr. Frick, and picking AGM was just the result of closing my eyes and sticking a pin in a list. The winners never question their luck, Mr. Frick. The losers are the ones who say they've been jobbed."

"You know," he said, "I like it. I really like it."

"Good."

"Just . . . just how will you work it with Hubbard, I mean if you decide you can handle it okay?"

He saw that sweet icy smile again. "Things run to pattern," she said flatly. "We will become terribly attracted to each other, and get around to admitting it, but we'll agree to fight it. Then I shall tearfully permit myself to be seduced, and it will be such a compelling and glorious experience that we won't be able to stop. We will agree that this will be our little stolen time of magical love, and when it is over, we will go our separate ways. But then, you understand, because I am so much in love I can't stand the thought of the heartbreak ahead, I will get a little drunk, and make some horribly slutty embarrassing scene in front of all the people he most wants not to know about his sneaky little romance Will that do it?"

"Dear God," Frick said, awed and humble. "That would sure do it."

"It's a scene I've played before. And the first two times I played it, I thought I meant it."

"One thing. Can anybody show up who'd . . . spoil the act?"

"I'm not notorious, Mr. Frick. I haven't taken on regiments. I'm not on a police blotter anywhere for anything. I have the quaint idea I resemble a lady."

"I only meant . . ."

"I'd say the odds are distinctly against it, certainly at the Sultana."

"Good."

"And if there was one of those little coincidences, I'm sure I could handle it very quietly."

"I'm sure you could."

"I suppose the most reasonable time and place is in the suite you mentioned, in another . . . fifteen minutes? Thats when you'll all be gathered. Say! Suppose the boss man, whoever he is, doesn't like the idea?"

"The boss man," Frick said with a barracuda grin, "is Mulaney."

"You can tip him off, then. I'll be playing it to the others as well as Floyd Hubbard, so even if Hubbard isn't there, tell your Mr. Mulaney to be . . . reasonably skeptical."

"Sure, Cory. I'll fix it up."

"I have the suite right? Eight sixty? I guess I'm dressed all right for that sort of thing. You could probably fit me into the dinner arrangements . . . if I decide I can help you."

"No trouble at all."

Miss Cory Barlund stood up, slung the oversized bag over her arm and began working her gloves back on. "I'll kill some time downstairs, and get to the suite about six thirty, if that sounds all right, Mr. Frick."

"It sounds fine. Just fine, only . . ."

"Only what?"

His lips felt slightly numb, and he knew it wasn't the drink. "What I mean to say, Cory honey, we've set up a sort of little business arrangement here and I don't have to get up there right on the dot, and I was thinking maybe we could . . sort of seal the bargain . . ." She devoted her entire attention to putting her gloves back on. He swallowed and said, "I . . . I could sweeten the pot a little."

She smiled at him, but something in her smile warned him to stay just where he was. "*Mister* Frick, let me set an imaginary scene for you. You walk into a good restaurant. You see me eating alone at a table. You've never seen me before in your life. Now how would you judge your chances of coming over, introducing yourself, and even being permitted to sit at my table and watch me eat?"

"Maybe not so good, but that would be because I wouldn't know . . ."

"What I am? You know what I am. At least you think you do." Her smile became more intense. "Let's make our relationship clear. At a rate of a hundred dollars a second, Mr. Frick, I wouldn't let an insect like you kiss the back of my hand."

He sprang to his feet and in a strangled tone said, "Listen, you! Listen to me!"

"Careful!"

"No high class whore is going to . . ."

The envelope of money appeared with the abruptness of magic, was slapped solidly across his mouth and fell to the floor at his feet. He looked stupidly down at it and then at Cory Barlund walking briskly toward the door.

"Hey!" he said. "Hey, wait!"

She had the door partially open before she stopped. She stood still for a moment, then slammed the door violently and turned and faced him.

"It seems to mean something to Alma," she said quietly. "And I seem to owe her more than a little. And your terminology is . . . rude but accurate. I'm a pretentious bitch, Frick. I'd like your apology."

"I'm sorry."

"So am I. Pick up the money and bring it to me."

She took it from him and put it in her purse again. "Try me again in ten years," she said. "By then I may

have lost the freedom of choice. That's supposed to be
the standard pattern, isn't it?"

She closed the door quietly. He walked back into the
room and called her every foul name he could think of.
She had left a faint trace of her perfume in the room.
He looked at the stain of lipstick on the two cigarette
butts she had left in the ash tray. There was a fainter
stain on the highball glass. There was a half inch of her
drink in the bottom of the glass. Without much conscious
thought he fitted his mouth to the pattern her lips had
left and drained what was left of her drink. When he
put the glass down he could taste the remote aromatic
pastiness of her lipstick.

It was ten minutes before six. On impulse he phoned
Alma. He let it ring twelve times before he hung up.

Four

THE suite was crowded and noisy by a few minutes after six. Hubbard stood by the open doors to the big terrace, nursing a tall drink and talking to Dave Daniels of the Chicago area and Stu Gallard of the Los Angeles district office about Cuba and Castro and foreign markets.

Gallard was saying, angrily, "Mitch brought back this half-horse motor he bought in Montevideo. Made in the USSR. The boys at Schenectady tore it down, and it was built damn good, I'm telling you. And for the price he paid for it, G.E. couldn't even buy the materials. It's a hit and run operation, and they figure on losing say a couple-hundred thousand to cripple a half-million dollar distribution system, and then they get the hell out. Just wait until they go to work on one of our . . ."

"Floyd! Floyd, boy," Jesse Mulaney bellowed, moving through the crowd. He came up and pumped Hubbard's hand and said, "Glad you could make it. Dave! Stu! How you boys? Both looking fine. Fine. Connie, honey? You know all three of these boys. Dave Daniels, Stu Gallard, Floyd Hubbard."

"Of course I do. So nice to see you here, gentlemen."

One of the road men came flurrying up with the Mulaneys' order, and in handing the drinks to them, managed to step on Hubbard's foot.

"I'm sorry," he gasped. "Geez, Mr. Hubbard, I'm terrible sorry."

"No harm done," Hubbard said.

"If you boys will excuse Connie and me, we've got to go shake every hand we can find before we settle down to any serious dissipation."

When Mulaney moved off, Hubbard noticed that neither Daniels nor Gallard made the slightest comment about him, and it was a significant departure from the normal routine, wherein somebody would say casually,

"A great guy," or "Jesse is looking fine." How beautifully the grapevine works, Hubbard thought acidly. The CIA should check into how it's done. A national organization, and it gossips more than the Podunk sewing circle. Fourteen members here of the big happy AGM family, and every single one of them, even to the road men, know I'm Hubbard the Hangman. Beware. Step easy or he may finger you too. And I've always wanted to be loved.

He made the small talk, and took the strategic sips of his drink, and was aware of trying to look and sound harmless and likable, and was ironically amused at himself.

About a half hour later, Charlie Gromer, one of the older road men, touched his elbow and said, "Excuse me. Mr. Mulaney wants to see you a minute in the next room."

The direct approach? he thought. Can't be. Not so soon.

He went into the bedroom Charlie indicated. Jesse was there, with Fred Frick of the local district and Cass Beatty of Advertising. An exceptionally lovely girl was talking to the three of them with considerable animation.

"There he is!" Jesse said. "Problems, Floyd. We figured maybe you could contribute a high-level policy point of view here. Miss Barlund, may I present Mr. Floyd Hubbard."

"How do you do, Miss Barlund. Jesse, before you give the young lady the wrong slant on things, let me say I consort with the brass. Some of them even say good morning to me when it's unavoidable."

"Run through it again for Floyd, Miss Barlund," Jesse suggested.

"It's sort of an off-beat idea, Mr. Hubbard, but I did sell it to Mr. Stormlander. He publishes Tropical Life; and I've been doing little free-lance articles for him. Everybody knows about conventions, but nobody knows very much about them, really. There's many misconceptions. And they're really a terrific industry down here. My idea is to take a typical company group at a typical convention, and do a sort of . . . well, a human interest thing. American businessmen at a convention and how they really and truly act—what they do, and what they think of conventions."

"Why us?" Hubbard asked. "Why AGM?"

"I guess I didn't go at it very scientifically. The companies are listed in the back of the program and I just picked one. I couldn't use the first one, because there's only one man here from that company. And the second one was too big. And the third one turned out to be Canadian. This one seems just about right, actually."

"Would you use actual names? And the name of the company?" Cass Beatty asked. "I didn't get clear on that."

"I'd *like* to," she said. "It would make it more real."

"It could get to be too real, couldn't it?" Hubbard said. "I remember a book a woman did about how they made a movie of *The Red Badge of Courage*."

She looked at him and the dark blue of her eyes seemed to change. He had the feeling she had noticed him for the first time and had found a reason for approval. He was surprised at how pleased he was.

"That was *Picture* by Lillian Ross," she said. "Golly, it wouldn't be that sort of thing. Tropical Life is more like . . . a sort of puff sheet. There's no reason you people couldn't approve the manuscript before I turn it in. You might even be able to use it in some of your company literature, if it turns out good enough. Really, all I want to do is just sort of mouse around, take a few pictures, ask people questions when they're not too terribly busy. I won't get in anybody's way, I promise."

"I don't know," Mulaney said. "I just don't know."

"Personally, I can't see anything out of line in it," Cass said. "It can't hurt anything, and we might get something we can use, maybe tear sheets to put in our direct mail stuff."

"How about credentials?" Frick asked.

"Tomorrow I could bring in a letter from Mr. Stormlander authorizing me to go ahead with it. I mean it wouldn't be a commitment on his part to really *use* it, because I am doing it on spec. But it would show he's interested."

"Sounds good enough for me," Frick said.

"Floyd? Cass? Any objections?"

"Hell, no!" Beatty said. Hubbard smiled and shook his head.

"You're in business, Miss Barlund."

"It's Cory, Mr. Mulaney."

"Freddy, you go grab a ticket book for Cory so she

can go to any of the events she feels like Floyd, you go on back out there and tell Bobby Fayhouser to shoo our people in here about three at a time and we'll brief them without busting up the party. Cory, we'll tell our boys to level with you and leave it up to you what to put in and what to leave out."

"Did many of the AGM men bring their wives, Mr. Mulaney?"

"You better call me Jesse. I brought Connie, and, Cass, you brought Sue. Anybody else?"

"That's the works then."

"I better get all the names down and the jobs," Cory said.

"Bobby Fayhouser has a list. You can copy it off."

Floyd found Bobby Fayhouser fixing drinks. He gave him the message.

"What?" Bobby said. "That girl is going to what?"

"Write a warm, heart-tugging story about how AGM goes to a convention."

"To be cast in bronze. Oh hell, excuse me."

"For what?"

"For the flip remark. They come out with no warning. I'm supposed to be eager and reverent."

Hubbard realized Fayhouser was not the dull, earnest young man he had appeared to be. "Cheer up. I've learned to live with the same problem."

"You, Mr. Hubbard! Doesn't it make people . . . uneasy about you?"

"All the time. But the way to handle it, Bobby, once it's said, don't let it just hang there, stinking in the sunlight. Say something very sincere."

"Something eager and reverent?"

"Then they're sure they didn't understand. Practice it."

"And one day I too can have a little stock option all my own? Uh. I have utmost confidence in the fairness with which every AGM employee is treated. Like that?"

"It could be smoother, but you've got the basic idea." They grinned at each other. Bobby trotted off with the drinks. Hubbard made himself a light one and carried it out onto the relative privacy of the terrace. The sea breeze was damp and had a salty smell. He heard the blur of voices behind him, a roar of surf, distant music, traffic sounds. The sun was gone and the sea was gray.

He looked for a star and found one and said the old rhyme. but did not know exactly what to wish for The words did not fit what he wanted Less confusion, more pattern, more meaning.

Jesse spoke at his elbow, saying, "Somehow I wish I was on that damn thing, going wherever it's going."

"On what?"

"Freighter out there, heading south."

"Oh. I see it. I was wishing too."

"Now what have you got to wish for, Floyd?"

"I don't know how to say it Better answers to better questions, I guess. The way I was when I was twenty and knew everything."

"What about the Barlund girl? You seemed a little dubious."

"Not really, I guess. I just had the feeling she's a little overspecified for the operation. As if that much girl should have something better to do. So I got the feeling maybe there's a gimmick in it someplace. But I guess not."

"Cass will check her out tomorrow." Mulaney chuckled. "Freddy's road men get short-winded when they get near her and their eyes bulge."

"Had a few symptoms myself, Jesse."

"Well, we'll see what she can do with this bunch of scoundrels. Hope she knows a little judo, for when it gets damp around here. I understand you got in pretty early?"

"And sacked out. They've been pushing me pretty hard lately."

Jesse clapped him on the shoulder. "Well, boy, there's nobody here to load any work on you, so take this chance to unwind. It'll do you a lot of good. Don't think you have to show up for every damn thing. There's nothing in the world duller than those clinics and morning workshops. You aren't a regular member of NAPATAN, so you won't get stuck on any committees."

"I don't know the first damn thing about selling anyway, Jesse."

"Aren't you supposed to know everything about everything?"

"What I actually know, and what they think I know, Jesse, is a pair of different shaped horses."

In the suite, Frick was giving Cory Barlund her book of tickets. He explained the mechanics of it to her, and then said in a lower tone, "You did great!"

"How delicious of you to tell me!"

"Don't needle me, huh? Is it a deal?"

"In the first three seconds, Frick, it was a capital Y Yes, and then it damned near turned into a no, but for a reason you couldn't hope to understand."

"I'm very stupid. Is it yes?"

"It's yes. And a very foolish yes, possibly. But yes."

"You think it'll be easy?"

"All you have to know is I'll give it a try."

At a little after eight they went down to the Arabian Room where the larger banquets were staged. AGM had two adjoining tables, each set up for eight. Because Jesse Mulaney had to be at the speaker's table, the addition of Cory Barlund created no problem. The table where she was seated also contained Cass and Sue Beatty, Connie Mulaney, Floyd Hubbard, Fred Frick, Dave Daniels and Stu Gallard. It was a round table near the platform. She sat directly across from Floyd. She was between Stu and Dave. Floyd was between Connie and Sue Beatty.

"That," whispered Sue, caught between indignation and admiration, "is one hell of a doll indeed."

"Yes indeed."

"Makes me feel the way I did when I was a fat child with braces on my teeth."

"You look fine, Sue."

"I wasn't fishing. You know, that girl comes on slow. She builds. The more you look, the more you see. Floyd, only a woman could know what kind of a total effort that takes, all the time and thought and care."

Sue Beatty clucked and shook her head. Sue was a hearty dominant woman in her middle thirties, heavy in hip and bust, solid but not fat, fond of bright colors, spiced foods, sweet drinks and lusty laughter.

There was so much noise in the room and so much conversation on the other side of the table they could talk with relative privacy.

"How old is she, Floyd? What would you say?"

"Twenty-two? Twenty-three?"

"How she would love you for that! Look at the backs

of her hands, dear man. And the base of her throat. Twenty-eight if a day. But doing very very well at looking twenty-two. Don't look at me like that. I know whereof I speak."

Floyd looked across at Cory in animated conversation with Stu Gallard. It was curiously disconcerting to think of Cory as being the same age as Jan. And his astonishment seemed a kind of disloyalty. It wasn't fair to Jan, of course. This Barlund girl apparently had nothing to do except keep herself as attractive as possible, and play around at little projects like this magazine thing. She had the sound and look and manner of money. Give Jan the same opportunity, and she could . . .

"Dave Daniels is moving in for the kill," Sue whispered. "Watch him."

Daniels, Floyd knew, had done more than his share of drinking before they left the suite. He was a big man, with all the simple devices of total vanity. Jan had met him once, after a series of meetings in Houston, and had placidly remarked that Dave Daniels was what you might get if you could cross Marshal Dillon with a horse.

Dave had broken up the Barlund-Gallard dialogue, and he was leaning close to Cory, talking in a low, intent, private voice, a half smile on his hard mouth, his eyes half closed. She listened without expression. He leaned closer and said a few words directly into her ear, laying his fingertips on her forearm as he did so.

Cory did not move her arm. He moved his fingertips back and forth in a tentative caress. She turned to face him more directly, smiled, and spoke to him for perhaps fifteen seconds. His mouth sagged open. He snatched his hand away. Cory turned back to Stu Gallard. Dave Daniels turned dark red, and the color faded to a curious sickly white. He pushed the food around on his plate for a few moments and then left the table abruptly.

Hubbard felt a warm delight. She glanced across at him, and he thought he saw one dusky eyelid shield one dark blue eye for a microsecond, but it happened so quickly he could not be certain he had not imagined it.

"Something tells me," Sue said, "that was a brush-off that'll have some kind of permanent effect. I guess she's had some practice."

"I wouldn't have thought it could be done," Hubbard said.

"Oh, it can be done," Sue said. "Even to the likes of Dave. You decide what a man holds most dear, about himself. Some little illusion. And then you stomp it."

Hubbard turned to Connie Mulaney on his right and said, "If friends don't stop this table-hopping to come and talk to you, Mrs. Mulaney, I'll never get the chance."

"Just when I get Freddy's shy little road men to start calling me Connie, you revert to formality, Floyd. Am I so darn imposing?"

"No. And I'm sorry. It's a sort of reversion to type, I guess. Protocol in the academic world. I hung around Cal Tech too long. If you are an instructor, and Smith is an assistant professor, and if you are twenty-two and he is twenty-three, by God, his wife is Mrs. Smith."

"I didn't know you'd taught, Floyd."

"I hated the teaching part, loved the chance to check out some of my wild ideas in those fine labs. Three years of it, then five years with an independent lab—research and testing with a commercial slant. Then over to GAE. Result, I feel like an imposter."

She tilted her head slightly, frowning, and said, "I guess everybody does, to a certain degree. There's some exceptions. Freddy, Dave Daniels . . . but the rest of us feel slightly displaced."

He realized once again that every time he was with this handsome and very human and very perceptive woman, he would marvel at her apparent love for and loyalty to a man like Jesse, who was such a big, loud, crude, mumbling extrovert. A lot of other people seemed to give Jesse love and loyalty, but so far Hubbard had been unable to discern any valid reason for it.

"I'll keep it to Connie from now on," he promised.

"Good."

"You certainly seem to know a sizable chunk of this group. How many would you say are here? Seven hundred?"

"At least. But Jesse and I don't know so many actually. We know the NAPATAN people better than the members of COLUDA. And, you know, there's been a lot of conventions in our lives. Jesse never forgets a name or a face, but a lot of the time I have to just smile sort of blankly and mumble. When the kids were small I was housebound, but now I get taken here and there."

"What will you do while this thing is going on?"

"Oh, shop and get some sun, and go to the more important things, and keep Jesse from getting too exhausted. Wifely work, Floyd."

The toastmaster huffed into the microphone, and there was a stirring and shuffling as the conventioneers and their ladies hitched their chairs around to face the platform. There was a traditional welcome to all delegates, and a thanking of the joint chairmen of the arrangements committee for their splendid work in setting the convention up so that it would run smoothly and effectively. There was an exhortation to all delegates to attend the workshops and panel discussions. The industry had had a successful year, all things considered. Of course there was dissension, but without irritation, oysters would never produce pearls. The exhibits this year were the finest ever. The program was the most exciting ever devised. And now there would be two addresses, one by Jerry Kipp, president of COLUDA, and the other by Jesse Mulaney, president of NAPATAN.

Kipp, a small, nervous, bespectacled man gave, with a total absence of humor, a speech apparently intended to create a great, selfless dedication and devotion to the industry, and its place in the great onward march of America.

Mulaney was introduced next. He stood at the lectern and after the applause had died down he let the silence grow. He looked out at the multitude with a slow owlish grin.

"I knew I'd have to do this. And I knew they'd fix me good. They put Bill and Jerry on first. By the time Bill was through, I'd crossed out half my speech. Jerry gave you the other half of my speech. So here I am standing up here like a nut.

"As you know, I'm the out-going president of NAPATAN, after the usual two years in this high office, where, according to honored precedent, I got the other fellows to do all the work.

"As I stand here, I see other ex-presidents out there. Fletch, Harry Mallory, Dix Weaver. They're honorary directors of NAPATAN now, same as I'll be. If there's anybody does less work than the president, it's an honorary director.

"During this convention, NAPATAN will elect a new president. Like the other officers and the members of the board, I have to go around pretending I don't know who it will be. That, too, is part of our tradition.

"Sixteen years ago I was elected to the board. Twelve years ago I was made recording secretary in spite of everything I did to wiggle out of it. Eight years ago I was made treasurer. Four years ago I became vice president. Two years ago, at the convention in Atlanta, I made my speech of acceptance as president, and that night I told my wife Connie that finally I could relax and start taking the bows for all the work the other fellows were going to do.

"I suppose that right here is the place where I should point with pride. I don't know. I've never had much trust in long lists of accomplishments. Oh, sure, we've got such a list. But to me, NAPATAN has been the way we can stand face to face . . . without agitating the anti-trust boys. And it has been these inter-company contacts which, over the twenty-four years since NAPATAN was founded, that have turned this industry from a cut-throat jungle into . . . into a respectable place to spend your life.

"Now don't get the idea everybody has given up sharp-shooting, and this has turned into a great big Bible school. Every company in this industry is still rough and tough and eager, because they have to be to survive. But NAPATAN has at least given us an arena where the rules are posted and nobody hits you after the bell.

"I don't know just how to say what I want to say to you people. To me . . . and I guess you know I'm a sentimental man . . . the breath of life itself is the strong, warm, honest contact between human beings."

He was silent for many seconds, and when he spoke again his voice was husky and uncertain. "Even if NAPATAN had failed at all the ambitious things it tried to do, I would still treasure my long association with it. Because . . . through this organization . . . I have been privileged to become a friend of . . . of some of the finest men our society has ever produced."

The applause was long and loud. People here and there began to stand, applauding, and soon the multitude was on its feet. Floyd had the uneasy feeling that perhaps too many people had underestimated Jesse Mulaney.

As the applause began to die he heard a man at the

table directly behind him. "Dix Weaver's speech. The same old crap, and it always works."

The man's neighbor said, "It was sixteen years he did nothing. Not two. You should hear Harry Mallory on that subject, Ed."

"How can a guy like Mulaney fake his way so far for so long? I heard that with the new team at AGM, they're finally catching up to that . . ."

"Ssshh!"

"Huh? Why're you . . . Oh."

Hubbard, as everyone began to sit down again, looked sidelong at Connie, hoping she hadn't overheard. But he knew at once that she had. She was staring down at the table, her lips compressed, her face pink, a tear in the corner of her eye.

"That was just what they wanted to hear, Connie," he said.

She looked at him and knuckled the tear away. She looked angry. "Certainly. That's Jesse's special talent, you know. Telling everybody exactly what they want to hear. That's the secret of salesmanship."

He made a forlorn attempt to turn it into a joke. "Not only salesmanship. Love and politics."

She seemed to study him. "It's a lot tougher, I imagine, to tell people the things they don't want to hear. But some people enjoy it. A certain special type of person."

"Connie, I . . . I don't think we ought to . . ."

She touched his hand. "Of course. I'm sorry."

The toastmaster made some closing announcements and adjourned the banquet meeting. Dave Daniels had returned for the speeches, but he left the moment it was over. It was ten thirty.

After the slow herd movement into the lobby, Floyd found himself with Cass and Sue Beatty. "What happens now?" he asked.

"Suite-hopping," Cass said. "A test of endurance. Everybody visits everybody else's suite. By my count there are twenty-three hospitality suites. One drink in each would be a masterful accomplishment. But many will try. Our little men are up there, bracing themselves for chaos. Miss Barlund shouldn't miss this sturdy tradition. She's over there with Stu. Sue, trot over and nab her and we'll make a group effort."

After an hour and a half of smoke, handshakings, short elevator rides, incompleted sentences and inadvertent animal contact, Hubbard worked his way across a fourth floor suite to where Cory was hemmed in by two admiring bald men.

"Miss Barlund," he said briskly. "They want you down at the main desk immediately. Come with me please."

He walked her briskly out of the suite, taking her glass from her and putting it on a table near the door. Fifty feet down the corridor they slowed their pace.

"Did it show that much, Floyd Hubbard?" she asked.

"Not too much. Your eyes kept rolling up out of sight and you kept dropping to your knees. But you got up every time."

"Where is this rescue party headed?"

They had arrived at the elevators. "It's midnight and your option, Cory. Want to try yet another suite?"

"Lord, no! You've seen one and you've seen them all." She looked at herself in the wall mirror in the elevator alcove. "I even look as if I smell like cigars. I want a dark little corner to sit in, with a place to rest my head, and a vodka stinger to drink slowly, and somebody who will talk to me and finish every sentence, and require very few answers."

"We take care of our journalists."

He found them a banquette corner in one of the smaller quieter bars in the hotel. It was called the Suez Lounge. A lean woman in silk harem pajamas played a listless, noodling piano. Cory took a sip of her drink and sighed and said, "And they're still up there, milling around. It's a scene I won't have to make twice. Do you think anybody is enjoying it, really?"

"Some of the drunker ones, maybe. But everybody thinks everybody *else* is enjoying it. But don't put that in your story."

"Sir, it is not my purpose to tear down honorable American institutions. I have a simple theme. Conventions are lovely."

"Is that what you want to write?"

"Not especially."

"So why don't you write about something where you can say what you want to say?"

"I'll tell you my horrid secret, Floyd. I'm strictly no talent. And I'm a horrible ham. I'll do anything to see my name in print. So I write little things people will buy. And once in a great while they actually do. Don't tell anybody, but this is my first crack at it in a couple of years." Her smile faded. She shrugged. "Call it busy-work. Restless female. Bored, I guess. Bored to the teeth."

"Because you don't have to earn the money?"

"Possibly."

"It wouldn't be alimony?"

She sipped her drink and put the glass down and turned toward him. In the shadowy corner he could see the gleam of her eyes and her teeth and a highlight of moisture on her lip.

"Rather than have you labor away at the personal history bit, Hubbard, suppose I just shovel it all out in one hideous chunk and then we can forget the whole thing forever. Okay?"

"If you want to. But I was only . . ."

"I'm a spoiled brat from way back. I went to a good school. I made a very bad marriage, and worked like a damn dog to keep it going, but it fell down dead. I have one child, defective, institutionalized. I have money coming in from a couple of places. I live well, and live alone, and try to like it. It helps to get all involved with idiot projects, like the one I'm on now. I am not the least bit sorry for myself. Now you can stop prying."

He sat for a full minute of silence. "I suppose two can play. I went to a good school, and I made a very good marriage, and we both work like dogs to keep it going, and it seems as if we will. I have two kids and one salary. I don't live as well as I would like to, except when I'm on the expense account, like now. I keep getting all involved in idiot projects, like the one I'm on now, but somebody else thinks them up for me. I very often feel terribly sorry for myself, without any good specific reason. Now you don't even have to start prying."

He could tell that he had startled her, topped her and amused her. "How about spoiled?" she asked.

"I would have liked to have been, but I was the third of six kids. The first and the last got spoiled."

"Floyd, darn you, I like you!"

"Right friendly of you, ma'm." They made a small ceremony of shaking hands. "But you weren't so friendly to Dave Daniels."

"Him! Ha! God, how I despise that type! But later I

thought that maybe I should have . . . pulled the punch a little bit. You see, Floyd, when I decided to do this, I knew very well that somebody was going to make the first pass. Somebody always does. I don't say that arrogantly. It's a fact of life I live with. And probably like. So I was braced to give the first one such a brush-off, the others would get the message. I didn't expect . . . that kind of a pass, exactly."

"From where I sat, it seemed sudden."

"It was."

"What was Dave's approach?"

"Do you really want to know? There are a certain percentage of men around, a very small percentage, who try the shock approach. It must work, or they wouldn't use it. I won't tell you exactly what he said. He started by saying we were going to take the first chance to sneak away from the rest of the group. He said conventions could be fun. Then he leaned closer and he . . . went anatomical, and told me the . . . kind of dimensions I could expect and how long he could make it last. I think I'm blushing."

"Good Lord! No matter how drunk I was, I couldn't ever . . ."

"I know you couldn't, dear. According to his script, I guess I was supposed to go all weak and dizzy and eager. So I just turned toward him and kept my voice down and said if that sort of thing attracted me, I'd have long since bought a Shetland pony. The conversation would be more attractive, and ponies seldom get pig drunk. Then I asked him why he was wasting his time at a convention when he could be cleaning up in the dirty movie business. I used my landed gentry voice. Ah, I can be a wicked bitch. I meant to shatter him, and I guess I did."

"He'll recover. He'll take an old-fashioned country remedy, and be just fine."

"What kind of a remedy?"

"A woman."

"Yes. Yes, of course. But I fear we shall never be friends."

"The kind of passes I make, Cory, they're so subtle nobody ever knows I've made one. The system has a lot of advantages. I get a little feeling of guilt, and nobody ever says no. But of course, nothing ever happens either."

"You mean you've made a pass at me?"

"It would spoil it if I told you. You see, you have to stay alert, and detect one when it comes along."

"And if I happen to detect one?"

"If you do, for heaven's sake, don't let on to me that you have. If I knew you knew, I'd run like a damned rabbit. I'm one of those married cowards, Cory."

"I'm glad you are, Floyd. It makes all this . . . sort of restful. We can kid around, and I don't have to stay on guard. It's rare and it's nice."

"Don't overdo it, now. Hell, let me feel a *little* bit dangerous, woman."

"But your wife *does* understand you?"

"With an eerie frequency."

"What's her name? What's she like?"

"Janice. Jan to almost everybody, including me. She's got a twenty-ninth birthday coming up, and we've been seven years married. The boy is four and the girl less than a year. Jan has gold-blonde hair and green eyes and a round face. She's bigger and heavier than you are. How tall are you?"

"Five-five."

"You look much taller than that!"

"It's because I'm a wraith. A hundred and five pounds. I'll even tell you the forlorn dimensions. Reading from the top they're thirty-one, nineteen, thirty-one. Symmetrical, no?"

"Not exactly. Thirty-one, thirty-one, thirty-one would be truly symmetrical. Putting that crazy nineteen in the middle is what saves it. Anyhow, Jan has a hell of a good figure, said he with husbandly pride. She's generally a placid gal, which works out fine because I'm inclined to blow up. Lately she hasn't been so placid. That's because I've had to leave her alone too much, and she has the idea I could get out of all this traveling. I could, but at the moment it doesn't seem to be the smart thing to do. You didn't ask for my problems. You asked about Jan. She is my nifty girl."

"It makes me feel like an urchin outside a candy store."

"You never feel sorry for yourself. Remember?"

"Any time I start to, all I have to do is remember the delights of *my* marriage. And suddenly you'd be surprised at how contented I get."

. "You should try again."

"Uh uh! I rode my little barrel over the falls, thank you. I survived, but not by much of a margin. Floyd, dear man, thank you for the drink and the talk. You can plant me in a cab, please. Tomorrow I'll be the earnest quester, and nail you down about what you really think about conventions."

Halfway through the lower lobby she stopped suddenly and turned, smiling, and said, "If you have time, and if it's possible to get anywhere near the ocean, ten minutes of sea breeze would blow the cigar smell out of this mop."

"I have time and there's an ocean around here some-where. I swear I've seen one."

They walked across the pool area and found an outside stairway that led up to the low flat roof of the furthest rank of cabanas. With most of the hotel lights behind them, they could see the phosphorescence in the waves. They stood side by side, looking over a low wall.

"One day," she said, "it ought to reach up with one hell of a big wave and yank all this gunky luxury right back out and drown it."

"Nature girl?"

"By instinct, but not habit." Suddenly she took her shoes off, put them on the wide railing and stood close to him, smiling up at him. "See? Five five. Not even that, actually. I lie a little. Five four and a little over a half inch."

"And you actually weigh seventy-two pounds, and the measurements are really nineteen, nineteen, nineteen."

"The *hell* you say, Hubbard." She came up on tip-toe, put her arms around his neck and sagged her weight on him. "A hunnert 'n five pounds of dreary broad."

She kissed him lightly, mockingly, and suddenly he was kissing her with a strength and fury he could not have anticipated. She fitted her slimness to him, strained to him, left her mouth soft for the breaking. The kiss ended and he was holding her close, whispering, "Cory, Cory, Cory, Cory." Her hands moved on his face and his throat, and she covered all the parts of his face she could reach with a hundred light quick kisses, making an audible, murmurous sound of contentment as she did so, until her mouth came back onto his, into a little more violence than before.

"You're not running," she muttered. "You're not running like a rabbit."

"Cory, Cory. God, you feel so sweet and good."

She thrust him away, snatched up her bag and shoes. "I better do the running, my darling. Right now it's the only thing that makes any kind of sense."

She fled more quickly than he would have guessed possible. He called to her, but she did not stop or answer. By the time he reached the bottom of the steps she was more than halfway across the pool area, moving fleetly through a confusion of colored spotlights and floodlights, between the tropical plantings, angling toward the flank of the tall pale hotel.

He slowed his pace and sat on a chaise near the pool and smoked a cigarette. He wiped her lipstick from his mouth. He looked at the sky, and went on up to his room.

He was wearily and dutifully brushing his teeth when the room phone rang. He hurried to the phone, half expecting long distance, half expecting some kind of family disaster.

"Floyd?" she said in a small wary voice.

"In that good school, were you by any chance on the track team?" He stretched out on the bed.

"Tennis, swimming, field hockey. No track team. I just got home. Just this minute."

"Did you ever get to put your shoes on?"

"Darling, I know you're keeping it all very light and gay so that this won't be an awkward sort of conversation, and I do treasure you for it. But I feel wretched, and I want you to please let me go on feeling wretched. And guilty."

"Why be guilty?"

"Because it was all so damn contrived, dear. When we started out, I didn't want to be put in a cab all of a sudden. I wanted to be kissed, and I meant to be kissed, and, damn it, I lied and fiddled around until I made sure that I did get kissed. You were like they say, a helpless pawn."

"We pawns make out pretty good."

"Floyd?"

"Yes?"

"It turned out to be more of a much than I'd planned on."

"I know."

"My mouth is bruised, and I keep getting these stupid trembling feelings like waves, and they go from my scalp right down to my toes and back up again."

"Best of luck."

"Tell me I did right to run."

"You did exactly right, Cory honey."

"And we have to leave it right there, don't we?"

"At the moment that seems like a cheerless prospect."

"Oh, I know. I know. But this hit a little too hard to . . . seem safe."

"Yes indeed."

"Somebody has to do the running."

"And you did it. You're a good sensible girl."

"Yes, damn me. Floyd?"

"Yes, dear?"

"I messed myself up. I don't want to mess you up too."

"Could you?"

"Help me, darn it! Tell me to stay the hell away from you."

"Sure. Stay away from me."

"Do you think it's going to be easy?"

"Certainly not. Now do me the same favor."

"Okay. Floyd, stay away from me."

"I'll give it a try."

"Did anything ever happen to anybody so sudden?"

"They say it does sometimes."

"Never to me."

"Or to me, before."

"Floyd, darling, we're just going to have to be terribly rational about it. Avoiding each other is just going to be tantalizing. The best thing we can possibly do is get together tomorrow, by the cruel light of day and talk it to death. What do you think?"

"Talking should do it. I'm still a coward."

"What were you doing when the phone rang?"

"Well, I didn't catch this girl's name, it all happened so suddenly, and it looks now as if she's given up and gone to sleep, but . . ."

"Floyd!"

"Actually, I was burnishing my fangs and thinking of you."

"What were you thinking about me?"

"Actually, I was trying to decide what to think about

you. I was trying to establish an attitude, I guess. But I was, and still am, a little too dazed to make very much headway with it. You see, Cory, this doesn't happen to Floyd Hubbard. It's out of character. One of the most beautiful women he's ever seen just doesn't fall into his arms. So Hubbard isn't ready. Right now he feels like a gay blade. Inside he's doing some swashing and a little buckling. He's got an imaginary waxed mustache. Hell, honey, he's flattered all to pieces, and half convinced they drugged you in that bar, and pretty certain that by tomorrow you'll laugh yourself sick."

"No, Floyd. No. Don't ever think that."

"The very first time I fell in love I was eleven, and she was a saucy little redhead named Ruthie. A very advanced ten. Sophisticated. I saved a buck thirty-nine and bought one hell of a big valentine heart full of candy and went shivering to her door that Sunday morning. She came to the door and I held it out and said, 'Duh . . . uh . . . duh . . .' She snatched it away, and her eyes lighted up and she gave me the most electrical smile in all the world and she squealed, 'Tommy sent it! Tommy made you bring it to me!' I hadn't put any card in it, so all I could do was walk slowly away."

"I could kill her! I could *kill* her!"

"The rest of the average story of my life goes like this. It obligated me to mend my wounds by bashing Tommy about. So I found a chance to pick a fight with him, and he beat the hell out of me. So you can see, Miss Cory, that when a beautiful woman swoons into my arms, my history makes me skeptical."

"I'm not beautiful. I'm a dreary, scrawny broad."

"And I am a dreary little husband, girl."

"Keep using that word tomorrow, Floyd. Husband. I despise poachers."

"Go to bed, Cory. Rest up for the battle. When are you coming over?"

"Midmorning, I guess. Sleep well, my darling."

"You too." He heard the sound of a sigh, a kiss, a clack of hanging up.

After the light was out he thought, Hubbard isn't ready, but she is. The thief said, "I was just walking down the street minding my own business and this here wallet bounced right into my hand."

But it would be so damned unfair. Jan has so little chance to compete in Cory's league. . . .

Yet he had a vivid textural memory of Cory's lips, of the sleekness and warmth of her back, of the small hardnesses of her breasts against his chest.

Who would have to know? Who could be hurt?

Five

ON the morning of the first full day of the convention, Connie Mulaney stood one step behind her husband and looked at him in the full-length mirror as he tied his tie.

"What are you cooking up, Jesse? I want to know."

"Cooking up? Who's cooking anything up, honey?"

"You have that look."

He spun around. "What kind of a look am I supposed to have? I'm under a hell of a lot of pressure. Maybe it shows. I can't help that. My God, Connie, I'm doing the best I can. I'm working hard. How about that speech last night? You saw how well it went over."

"You did very well, dear. You always do."

"I've got to run a committee meeting, starting at ten."

"So you've been telling me." She reached and adjusted the knot of the tie, patted it, stepped back. "That'll have to do."

As they walked toward the nearby elevators he said, "How'd you get along with Floyd Hubbard? I saw you were sitting next to him."

"He's a very nice boy, Jesse."

"Did he seem to like my speech?"

"He seemed impressed."

They stood waiting for the elevator. "Somehow, I can't get to know him."

"Why not, dear? He seems easy to know."

"For one thing, he won't let his hair down. He lays back. Weak drinks and damn few of those. He's one of those guys who'd check and raise. A damn sandbagger if I've ever seen one."

As they got onto the elevator she said, "Now, dear, a man can be entirely human and still not go hog crazy at a convention."

"Like our grandson says, honey, that fella bugs me."

"I don't see why he should."

61

"No matter where I am, I got the feeling he's seven feet behind me and off to one side, listening and watching."

When they were seated at a table for two and had ordered breakfast, he brought Hubbard up again. "He said he doesn't know anything about selling, but he's certainly memorized all that crap in the GAE management manual. One thing he asked me last night. He wanted to know what I thought about the idea of changing over to dividing up the sales force by products instead of into geographical areas."

"What did you tell him, dear?"

"I just told him we'd been up one side of that and down the other up in New York, and I think a good knowledge of an area, and a good warm personal relationship with all potential customers makes more sense than all this crap about knowing one part of the line inside and out. I told him my men are salesmen, not technical consultants."

"What did he say?"

"I guess he didn't say much of anything, but I guess he saw my side of it. Then he brought up some egghead idea of teaming up an engineer and a salesman, but I knocked that down quick. I told him that the quickest way to kill a sale is bring in the technical boys too early, because they can always think of a dozen reasons why an installation won't work out. I say nail the sale down, then *make* the damn thing work."

"I guess he's anxious to learn from you, dear."

"If he'd listen, I could teach him one hell of a lot. But I wish to God he'd stop working for a couple of minutes. If he'd have six drinks and find him a friendly little girl, he'd get a more tolerant attitude toward the sales division."

"And give you a chance for a little gentle blackmail?"

"Who said anything about blackmail?"

"Don't raise your voice, darling. And don't look so innocent and indignant. Remember me? I've been around a long time. I've seen you work it before at conventions. I remember that fearless state senator in Nashville that time."

Mulaney grinned. "The one that was going to nail us on kickbacks? Hell, yes! By the third day he was following me around like a little puppy dog, because I'd opened up a brand new world for that poor love-starved man."

"It won't work with Floyd, dear. Maybe he isn't righteous, but I think he's terribly careful."

They ate in silence for a few moments. "At least," Jesse said in a slightly surly tone, "we've got the top exhibit in the place."

"Have we?"

He dropped his fork with a clatter and stared at her. "What's wrong with it, Con? You saw it. You saw the attention it's getting."

"And I saw a look of pain on Hubbard's face, dear. What's getting the attention? AGM products? Or those cheap twins wiggling their butts in unison? It's typically a Freddy Frick idea. Vulgar, sensational and sexy. Even Cass is visibly uneasy about it. It doesn't exactly tie in with the magazine campaign, does it?"

"Woman, this isn't a magazine. This is a convention."

"And anything goes? Anything for a laugh?"

He glanced at his watch, glared at her and stood up. "I've got to go. Sign the check. Thanks for the big boost to the morale, honey."

She watched him stride out of the restaurant. Her eyes were stinging, and she tried to smile. The dear, dear vulnerable fool. Met him when he was a drummer. Day coaches, rooming houses, the heavy sample case, the small stores in the sleepy towns. And so little had changed, actually. The cigars were more expensive. But the jokes and the laugh were the same. And those truly horrid suits in that electric blue he loves, and the wide silk ties, like photographs of fireworks. But he isn't mean. Thank God, he isn't mean. He's just scared.

On that same morning, Farber of GAE flew to Houston from New York on a quick inspection tour and conferred with John Camplin, the new executive vice president of the American General Machine Division of GAE. They were both trim tailored men in their early forties, so much the same type they gave the impression of being related.

After the more urgent problems had been talked over, and decisions reached, Farber said, "You're shaping it up faster than anybody expected, John. And it takes me off the hook for insisting on moving you into the hot seat."

"Nice to hear, Harry. There's a long way to go. It

wasn't only dead wood, it was dry rot. With a couple of exceptions, the new team is working out."

"How about sales? Frankly, that's the only place where you haven't moved as fast as I thought you would. Why haven't you gotten Maloney out of there? Recruiting trouble?"

"His name is Mulaney. No. I've got a good man lined up to come over with us as soon as I say the word. I had to steal him."

"Then why are you dragging your feet?"

"It's sort of a PR problem, Harry. He's president of one of the industry associations. He's at the convention right now, where they elect a new president. We wouldn't have looked too good giving him the ax earlier. And he's a stubborn old bastard. He might have gone to the convention anyway, and made his speech and hit us over the head with it."

"That makes sense."

"He goes next week. Plaque, citation, tears and full retirement."

"Full?"

"He's only two years off it now, so what does it cost for a gesture? An extra seven hundred a year. We did the same thing for Lane, remember? It buys a little loyalty, and leaves me with no guilt. In fact, one of my boys is down at that convention making a final confidential report on him."

"Good God, John, what do you need with another report? That man has never . . ."

"Whoa! I sent Hubbard over there, for a good reason."

"Hubbard? Hubbard? Is that the one you were telling me about in New York a couple of months ago. Some kind of technical fellow?"

"Metallurgical engineer. I called him in and conned him. I told him we still weren't certain about Mulaney. I said the evidence was against the man, but he was reputed to do us a lot of good at conventions and things like that. I told him his report would be the final deciding factor in whether we live out the two years with him, gradually transferring responsibility and authority or get rid of him right now."

"With a man like Mulaney, you can't take things away piece by piece. He'd bitch up the whole . . ."

"I *know* that, Harry. And so do you. This Floyd Hubbard was one hell of a find. He's got first class organizational instincts. He's shrewd about people. He can work like a horse and shrug off the pressure. I've been sticking him into some very hairy situations, and he's done damn well. But they've been office-hours problems, without the social overtones. I have one doubt in my mind about him. I don't know if he's rough enough. I have a hunch he is, but he has yet to find that out about himself. Do you understand?"

"You've set him up?"

"Like a target. Mulaney has a smarter wife than he deserves. And he has a merciless bunch of old buddies working for him. And I made sure the word got spread around that Hubbard was sent to do the final hatchet work on Mulaney. So I'll find out what some new pressures can do to my boy. If he weasels the report, I'll know the basic toughness isn't there. I'll still have some use for him, but it'll be limited. There's only one answer he can give me, but he doesn't know that Mulaney is out whatever he says. If Hubbard makes like a sailor on a pass, I'll know about that, too, and put a lid on his future accordingly. But if it works out, Harry, I'll have me a man better than . . . Harris or Lunt or Tomaselli. I'll have me a man that'll be pressing me hard in a few years, so hard maybe I'll wish I never found him in this outfit."

"In some ways, John, you are a mean son of a bitch."

Camplin grinned. "I'm doing a mean job, thanks to you. Hubbard would understand exactly what I'm doing. This is a hardness test, Harry. That would be right up his alley. A piece of bar stock can look just fine. But you don't know what you've really got until you take it into the testing lab and see what it reads on the scale. The world is full of sweet bright young men, Harry. With big warm hearts. Group-adjusted. Group-oriented. Christ, we recruit them in carload lots. But if you ask any one of them to fire another, he'll turn ashen and collapse. I sent Hubbard to Seattle to see if he had any ideas about tightening up that warehouse operation. A week later he sent me a wire from Los Angeles. It said, 'Close that crummy mess up there and consolidate here. Figures follow.' I wired him back. 'Close it yourself.' He wired me. 'Send me a lawyer.' Two weeks later he came wandering in, grinning, and told me that he'd discovered the secret of going without sleep. Just never

get within forty feet of a bed. Accounting says the move
will save us upwards of a hundred thousand a year, even
including the additional freight charges."

"Isn't that enough? Did you have to con him on
Mulaney?"

"I don't want to be almost positive. I have to be dead
certain."

At ten-thirty Cory Barlund was drinking black coffee
with Alma Bender in the paneled kitchen of Alma's apart-
ment. Had Alma's hair not been dyed a dark and rather
poisonous red, she could have posed for a granny's
baked-goods advertisement.

"Pete Stormlander will have the letter ready for me
to pick it up," Cory said. "Big problem. If I asked him,
he'd type up his own suicide note for me and bring it
across town on his hands and knees. Through traffic.
He sickens me."

"Cory, dear, you are in your usual happy frame of
mind. And your lovely eyes are just a little puffy."

"Somehow I didn't sleep very well. What I should have
done was keep on walking right out that door when that
Frick animal started panting and drooling."

"Freddy isn't that bad, sweetie. But you don't think
you'll have any trouble with the Hubbard fellow?"

"He's a sitting duck, Alma." Cory looked at the older
woman pleadingly. "But he's such a *good* man. Such a
damned *good* man!"

"But this saint will climb into the sack quick enough,
won't he?"

"Yes. But I've got to provide all the rationalizations,
and all the little accidents, and take it all off his shoulders. There's a strong physical attraction. Stronger than
. . . anything in a long time. Damn it, I want to be girly
about it. You know? Sweet and sighing and submissive,
and let myself cry if I want to."

"Wouldn't that just make it worse?"

Cory sighed. "Probably. So he'll get the complete de-
luxe deal. But one little bonus I'm giving myself, Alma.
No faking. I'm going to get just as much as I give and
maybe more."

"Which, as you damn well know, is stupid and dangerous. You act half in love with this convention clown
already, sweetie. Do you want to make it worse? The

smart whore hates every customer, and that's all he is, you know."

"He doesn't know it."

"But he'll guess it sooner or later."

"I hope to God I never have to see his face after he does."

"Cory, baby, how come you have such a talent for getting all screwed up?"

"Screwed, at least."

"Don't talk smart and dirty in my home, thank you."

"I'm sorry, Alma. I'm just upset about this. Sometimes, lately, I think I'd have been better off if you . . . hadn't happened along when you did."

"That's a hell of a thing to say to me!"

"I shouldn't have said it."

"You're more problem than any other four girls I've ever worked with, sweetie. If I had better sense, and if I didn't like you, I'd have let you go it alone a long time ago. And with your judgment, you'd be working the five o'clock in a cocktail bar by now, shook down by every cop in the precinct and clapped up three times a year and ready to go off a causeway bridge. And such a hell of a waste that would be." She grasped Cory's hand. "Don't try to dream, sweetie. Don't try to sell yourself that heart-of-gold routine. You got a heart like a stone or you wouldn't be in the trade. Take your fun if you have to, but I'd say you'd be better off without it. Just keep in mind that this saintly man is hot to put it into a girl the second day he knows her, and he and Freddy Frick are a lot more alike than they are different from each other. And remember you'll be doing a favor for an old friend of mine."

"Mulaney seems to be a slob."

"Of *course* he is, sweetie. Of *course* he is. But he's been generous to me, and I kind of like the old bastard. So you just drive this Hubbard half out of his mind, and then make a jackass of him in public." She lowered her voice. "You know what I've always told you. Pretend he's Ralph."

Cory snatched her hand away, closed her eyes, swallowed hard and swayed in the chair for a moment. Her color returned and she opened eyes like blue porcelain, a deep, hard, inhuman blue. "I'll spoil him," she whispered. "Ah, I'll spoil him."

"Don't look at him like that, Cory. It even scares me."

Cory stood up. "Off to do battle. You're right, of course. There's no dreams, no heart of gold. Just a stone heart, and whore tricks, and some more lies, and what's between the legs."

"You'd be more content if you'd do less thinking."

"Don't you think I try to stop? I've got to go."

"One thing, Cory. You made a bargain. You'll go through with it all the way, not just half of it."

"Don't worry about it."

"I wouldn't want to have to send Ernie around to straighten you out again. I like you best of all, sweetie, and it hurt me to have to do that to you."

"I said you don't have to worry about it!"

"Don't shout at me in my own home, darlin'. Now be off, and don't do all that thinking."

Cory paused in the doorway. "What about . . . if after this I decide to quit."

"But you won't."

"I might, Alma. I really might."

"Like you've done before? How many times? Six? Eight? Stop wasting your pretty breath, girl. You like things nice. You like them too well. And what other way is there to get them so easy? You're lazy, girl. Whore lazy. Talking of quitting is just another dream. You'll make your good living on your back until your looks are too far gone, and you'll never stop thinking you're a little too good for this kind of work. But just what the hell else are you good for? You better go now because at the moment I'm getting a little sick of you."

"Bitch!" Cory whispered. "Fat mean bitch!"

Alma got up and lumbered toward her, and Cory fled. Alma went back to her coffee, smiling mildly. She wished she had the talent to write a book on the trade. Case histories, sort of. Cory would be Miss C——. The past four-year history would show that quite often a sensitive, intelligent girl who is determined to destroy herself can be made into a profitable property. The self-hate and the man-hate has to be put to work. They're hard to handle, but they command a good price. And they seem to last a lot longer at top rates. The dim, placid, little sluts, they control easy, but they go downhill·fast, and no matter how fresh and sweet they look when you

start them out, they're usually ready to be wholesaled off
in no more than three years, that is, if you want to keep
a class clientele.

At the Sultana the executive offices were located on
the mezzanine floor and in an office area behind the registration section. However, the public relations director
and his small staff were quartered in an office suite at
ground level at the far end of the Convention Hall. There
were three offices, a large workroom, a dark room, a
printing and duplication room, and a private, luxurious
bar-lounge setup. The offices and work areas looked out
toward the pool and cabana area, and even, if one
stood in exactly the right place in the largest office, toward the ocean, visible as a narrow vertical ribbon of blue.
The private bar was the invention of Alan Amory, the
director of public relations for the Sultana. It was
called the Hideaway Club. Drinks were on the house,
but the service hours were limited—noon to one P.M.,
five to seven. All advance registrations and sudden check-
ins were scrupulously monitored by the PR staff and
checked against Celebrity Service, Who's Who and Dun
and Bradstreet. A selected few were issued metallic mem-
bership cards. Amory had also done quite well by quietly
delivering cards to extra-special celebrities who unfor-
tunately happened to register at other hotels in the area.
The name of the club, plus the "members only" designation, often awakened sufficient curiosity.
At eleven o'clock Alan Amory stood alone in his office
in a mood of listless depression. He was a willowy man in
rust-colored silk slacks, a pale yellow Italian sports shirt.
He had a bland oval face, thinning mousy hair, and
some rather precious mannerisms. Yet, over the years,
all those female employees who had achieved a false
sense of security by privately classifying him as queer
had, sooner or later, become acquainted with the enorm-
ity of their error.
The sounds of business which came from the workroom did not hearten him. He knew it was all dog work,
standard releases to hick papers regarding the local activ-
ities of one of their prominent citizens, heavily larded
with Sultana promotion, and complete with the glossies
taken by his staff photographer. The whippety-click of
the high-speed mimeos seemed joyless also, signifying

only that he was sending gimmicked copy to a thousand indifferent city desks on what he had analyzed to be a thirty-two to one chance of use. The hotel was jammed with nobodies. They'd cut the nut on entertainment in the public rooms of the hotel. There wasn't even anybody worth a Hideaway card, and nobody due that was worth one for the next ten days. Lately, he thought, it's like trying to puff a body and fender shop. Maybe turning down Vegas was the worst mistake of my life.

He had once been a radio tenor, of some small romantic vogue, and when the voice had started to go, he had begun managing a few people, starting with an ex-wife. In the early fifties he had learned that if he developed somebody hot he'd always be squeezed out by MCA or Morris, so he had moved over into the night club thing and then into hotels.

Rick DiLarra came bustling into Amory's office. DiLarra was a swart, bursting, beetling man, full of a conviction and enthusiasm that was almost plausible. He was the convention director for the Sultana.

Amory turned slowly and looked at DiLarra with mild distaste. "Where were you, sweets?"

"Honest to God, no more than three minutes ago I heard you wanted to ask me something, Alan. I was trying to get the lighting straightened out for . . ."

"What the hell have you got over there, sweets? Buggy-whip dealers?" Amory drifted over to his flight-deck desk and sagged into a plum leather armchair.

DiLarra perched a chunky hip on a faraway curve of the desk and said earnestly, "No, this is one of the better ones, honest to God. A hell of a lot better than that last bunch. It's a heavy industry crowd, and every cash drawer in the place is getting well. Is something wrong?"

"I got a call from a clown I know slightly. Stormlander his name is. He publishes a thing called Tropical Life. We make a due-bill deal on a small ad once in a while, I understand. He called just as a matter of courtesy, to say a broad will be in the house doing a spec coverage on one of the outfits in your convention. Something called AGM. That mean anything, sweets?"

"Honest to Christ, Alan, if I started worrying about what initials mean, I'd go nuts."

"Stormlander says give her cooperation if she asks for it, and if it's something he can use, we'll get tear sheets in advance. I thought you'd maybe know something about it."

"I haven't heard a thing."

"I wrote the girl's name down here. Cory Barlund. That mean anything either?"

"Absolutely nothing, Alan."

"I thought I'd better check it out with you before I waste time checking it a different way."

"Some kind of trouble?"

"I don't know. A small bell rings. I've got the idea she was lined up out of the Hideaway a couple or three times in the past couple of years. But I can't remember who it was through. I think she's a little high-style piece for the top dollar, and maybe part time rather than regular—that is if it's the same kid. Rest easy a minute while I check."

Alan Amory used his direct line, equipped with a mouthpiece which made it impossible for DiLarra to hear a word he said. After Amory got his party he talked for about a minute and a half and then hung up.

"I was right, but I'm not as worried as I was."

"Why should you have been worried anyway?"

"After all these years you're still innocent? A call girl comes into the house all set so she can pretend to be something else, all cleared with me in case somebody gets suspicious, and you should know right away somebody is being set up. It could be my business, Rick. There's money in that herd of nothings you've got over there. So suppose it was a high-level badger game bit? And the sucker doesn't stand still for it. And it becomes a police and newspaper thing. That would be wonderful public relations, sweets."

"So why aren't you worried so much now?"

"Because this chick is on Alma Bender's list, and that's a solid guarantee of no trouble. No blackmail, no disappointments. When we got anybody here who could be done a lot of damage and who'll go for the rate, I play it safe and use Bender, and there's never been a kick yet. Hey, sweets! Now I know how it is I remember the name of that chick. Cory Barlund. Sure. Remember the honorable congressman from Indiana, over a year ago? The youngish one hiding out down here so he wouldn't have to testify and embarrass a friend?"

"Almost two years ago."

"Nice guy. He got lonesome. I used Bender and got him that chick. He flew down here I swear five times trying to get her again, by name, but she never would make the return match, and every time he got a no, I thought he'd break into tears. That's why the name was familiar. Otherwise, who the hell would remember their names? And why? I feel safe, but I think I'll check it with Alma Bender anyhow, just to be sure Barlund isn't going this one alone."

"Anything I should do?"

"No, sweets. If it's sour I'll let you know and find some way to handle it."

DiLarra stood up. "One thing that always gets me. Why do they buy it? Why do they pay so much? God, Alan, this town is so full of . . ."

"Use your head, sweets. Sure, any guy who isn't a complete monster can kill himself down here on random tail, but he is always running into problems. Sometimes she turns out to be a teaser, or a lush, or even sick. Or she wants to fall in love, and that's a problem. Or she's two months along and is looking for somebody to set up for the marriage bit. Or she's a nut. Or the cops want her. And even when you have none of those problems, it still takes a lot of time and talk setting it up. And maybe, if everything else is fine, you end up with somebody with no talent for it. The busy, important man, sweets, does better with a high-level pro. All the questions are answered before you start. If he wants to do the town, he knows she'll look good enough and dress well enough to take anywhere. And she won't get plotzed or chew with her mouth open or leave him for somebody else in the middle of the evening. He knows just how the evening is going to end up, and he knows she'll be good at it, and he knows there won't be any letters or phone calls or visits a couple of weeks or months later. It's efficiency, sweets. Modern management methods. And these days, if he travels first class, he's working on a two-to-one chance she'll have a college degree."

"Are you selling me?"

"In any game in the world, Rick, never bet on the amateurs, because you'll never know what the hell they're going to do."

In the murmurous, echoing emptiness of the Convention Hall, seven separate workshops were in progress. In private meeting rooms, committees were at work. In the Convention Hall men wandered away from the study groups when their interest lagged, and kibitzed other groups. The voices of the speakers, unamplified, droned in a sleepy, uncoordinated chorus. Men wandered and glanced at each other's badges of identity, and joined in groups of two and three and four to talk in low voices about how drunk who got and who had what lined up. They asked about each other's families, told stories about other conventions, exchanged gossip about who was going to be promoted and who was on his way out.

The hospitality suites were muted with a recuperative quiet, the stains removed, the liquor replenished. Of seven hundred delegates, perhaps three hundred would sleep until noon, and there was another much smaller group which was still out somewhere in the city, their hotel beds unused. Hangovers ranged from mild dull headaches to repetitive, uncontrollable nausea.

There was a constant trickling traffic through the exhibit ramp. Delegates picked up brochures and pamphlets, accumulating bright glossy assorted stacks which would clutter a bureau top for several days and then be dropped in the room wastebasket at the time of packing. At the AGM display, Bunny and Honey, in starchy, brief little cotton sunsuits, wriggled, pranced, smirked, passed out the literature, activated the displays, chanted the memorized answers to anticipated questions and, from time to time, when a group of at least ten had accumulated around the display, they would go into the routine, much like a prolonged television commercial, which Tommy Carmer had made them learn.

Several of the corporations, including AGM, had rented pool area cabanas for the duration of the convention. These were the gathering places for the rather small contingent of wives of delegates. They lay on the casually grouped chaises, greased themselves constantly, gossiped, practiced corporate gamesmanship, ordered tall rum drinks and made agonizing decisions about what to do with the rest of the day—such as to go shopping or take a nap or play cards.

Amid the forenoon silences on the third floor, north wing, several salesmen of a company which makes large industrial pumps, were in danger of strangling on their

own attempts to laugh without making a sound while they
played an innocent game on one of their shyer associates.
They stood outside the door of the company suite looking along forty feet of corridor to where the most in-
veterate practical joker of the group stood, tensed and
furtive, within reach of one of the big aluminum house-
keeping carts. The cart stood outside one of the rooms.
The door of the room was ajar. At intervals of almost a
minute, the joker would reach out, grasp the pull-bar of
the cart and shake it, so that the soiled glasses and the
containers of cleaning materials would jingle and clatter.
Each time he did so, the observers would clutch each
other and make small groaning sounds as they tried to
stifle their intense amusement.

Earlier that morning, an enterprising one in the group
had discovered that the maid for that end of the corridor was available for special service, at ten dollars a
throw. She had obliged the others of the group in turn,
all except the shy one. The romantic aspects of it left
something to be desired. She was a tall Austrian girl
with ginger hair, a sharp nose, bulging blue eyes, a turkey
neck, a heavy accent, meager breasts and round heavy
hips.

There were rules to be obeyed, ja? The door, it has to
be open. The cart, it must be outside door always. And
the cleaning schedule, it must be kept, ja?

After she had decided to take the risk of a multiple
income, she had stowed her panties under the stack of
clean towels on the housekeeping cart. She was too much
in terror of the housekeeper to risk removing her gray and
white nylon uniform. So she hitched it high, and
performed with a strenuousness partially motivated by
panic, and kept her eye on the room door at all times.

They had, with difficulty, talked the shy one into taking his turn. He had been very dubious about the open
door.

Suddenly the joker tensed, whirled and came sprint-
ing soundlessly along the corridor. The five salesmen
erupted into the suite, gasping, hugging themselves. The
joker, eyes streaming, said, "She . . . she cussed him out
in kraut . . . and she . . . she said she couldn't waste
. . . any more time. Shh, you guys. He's coming."

The shy one walked in. He looked troubled. They
asked him how it was. "Damn it. Every time I'd get set,

some goddam noise in the hall would . . ." One of the salesmen could contain himself no longer and burst into a high wild guffaw that started the others going. The shy one stared at them with growing comprehension, then gave a roar of anger and charged the nearest one and made an almost alarmingly successful attempt to hurl his tormentor through the nearest window. At the expense of one split lip and one minor nosebleed, they finally pinned him down and sat on him until he had cooled off.

Out at the Pagoda Bar, beyond the Olympic pool, a florid sales manager decided after three Bloody Marys that he couldn't face the idea of lunch, and the only thing to do with his hangover was take it back to bed and hope it would be gone by late afternoon. He looked at all the flesh exposed to the sun and fancied he could hear it sizzling. Two couples went away, leaving just two people at the bar for the moment, the sales manager and a dark-haired woman in a white bathing suit. She was deeply tanned, her shoulders gleaming with oil and perspiration. She was plain but pretty enough, and she looked bored. She was four stools away. He looked at her thighs, where the brown flesh bulged as it escaped the stricture of the swimsuit fabric. He was conscious of her having glanced over at him a few times. Never when you want one, he thought. Always when you don't. On a weary impulse, courting rejection, he took his room key out of his pocket, held it under the level of the bar, rapped it against the wood to attract her attention, then held it so she could read the number on the plastic tag, looking at her with a fixed stare of inquiry and defiance.

She looked away quickly, her lips thinning, her face darkening slightly. He felt relief. He signed the check, left a tip and turned to go. The woman coughed. He turned and looked at her. She stared at him without expression and gave him a single abrupt nod of agreement. As he started the enormous journey to his room, he focused his mind hopelessly on the memory of the bulge of thigh, trying to summon up visions of delight, anticipation, but feeling only the weariness of too many hotels, too many conventions, too many million miles back and forth across the land, too many women, so many that now the memories of all of them had merged at last into a single unstimulating vision, white, gasping, fatty, strap-marked and secondhand.

Six

LITTLE Miss Cory Barlund came out of the eighth floor elevator at eleven thirty, paused to orient herself, and then began walking down the carpeted corridor that led to the AGM suite. She had the lithe walk of a model, all control, nothing sexy, nothing obvious. She wore her best "little nothing" dress, a junior dress, sleeveless, with a high collar, beltless, of such a calculatedly casual fit that it clung where and when it should, and swung free when it should, clinging and touching and releasing in the rhythm of her chin-high stride and the small movement of her toffee hair. The dress was the color of milk sherry. Her shoes were white and her small purse was white, and she wore gloves that matched the sherry dress perfectly. There were little gold buttons in her pierced ears. Her nylons were sheer as cobwebs, and latched to a riband of garter belt. Her panties were lace and her half bra was an A cup, and the aromatic redolence of the perfume behind her ears and on her wrists and between her breasts was forty dollars the ounce.

She moved down the corridor and kept herself from thinking by focusing on a pleasant sensual awareness of the slight movements of the fabric touching her body and the rhythmic little thump of the camera pack against her hip, dangling from the narrow strap over her right shoulder.

When she was more than halfway down the corridor, a door not far in front of her opened and Dave Daniels came out. He started to close the door, then noticed her. Unshaved, he was in shirt sleeves, a cigarette in the corner of his mouth. She nodded coldly and tried to move around him, but he blocked her passage.

She backed up a few steps and said, "Let me by, please."

"After I tell you you're not kidding me a bit. I got an instinct. I always know the score."

"Did you start drinking again? Or are you still drunk, Mr. Daniels?"

"Come on in and talk it over."

"Not today. Not any day."

He reached for her but she backed up swiftly. She said calmly, "You're an idiot, Daniels. How much do you think you can get away with? I took voice lessons for five years. I know how to breathe and how to project. If you touch me, I could make a noise that would open every door on this floor. And if you bother me one more time, I'm going to explain to all the rest of them that I have to drop the article because you're making it too difficult for me."

Daniels leaned against the corridor wall. "So what will work?"

"Give up."

"But now I got you on my mind."

"And that will be a terrible source of worry and concern to me, Mr. Daniels," she said, and walked past him and on down the corridor. He watched her intently until she turned into the suite, and then he went back into his room, lifted the bourbon bottle and drank from it until an involuntary gag closed his throat. "I'm Dave Daniels," he said thickly. "I never miss. One way or another, I never miss. Never have. Never will."

It was quarter of twelve when Floyd Hubbard, nearing the open door of the AGM suite, heard and recognized Cory's laugh. Though her voice was light and almost frail, her laugh, as he had noticed the previous evening, was full-bodied, earthy, as if she had borrowed it from a more vigorous woman. The laugh moved his heart up into the peak of his chest, and he swallowed it back down.

She was in the suite with Bobby Fayhouser, Charlie Gromer and Les Lewis, and she was taking a picture of the three road men against the background of the small AGM exhibit which had been set up in the suite. The flash attachment made its quick white flicker of light, and she turned and smiled at him, winding the film as she turned. "Hi, Floyd. I want one of you too, even though I don't know what you do yet. Bobby and Les have been telling me that for their jobs, AGM

she was at an adjoining table. He felt vaguely irritated that she should be having such an obviously hilarious time talking to Carmer on one side of her, and Cass Beatty on the other. The two AGM wives were not there. He was seated between Charlie Gromer and Dave Daniels. Gromer was too wary of him to want to say very much, and Daniels was so woodenly drunk it required all his concentration to appear undrunk. The speaker was reasonably amusing, but his talk was too long.

As the big room emptied, he kept an eye on Cory, and moved in from the flank after she had reached the lobby. Carmer seemed reluctant to part company with her, but she solved it by putting her hand out and saying, "It was such fun talking to you, Tom. I hope it'll happen again soon."

As she turned to Floyd she said, "I knew it was you standing there. I've acquired a brand new seventh sense, darling. I've known just where you've been every moment."

They moved over toward the wall. "Where do we start killing it with conversation?" he asked. "In a bar? By the pool? Some public place."

She tilted her head to the side. "I've got to find a place to change film, dear. I'm at the end of a roll. It's very sensitive. I have to have complete darkness. I can change it by touch. I looked in the girls' room, but there's no place there. There's no window in your bathroom, is there?"

"No."

"We could go up there first, and then think of a place to talk."

"How smart is that, Cory?"

"You mean being seen?"

"No, I don't mean being seen, and you know it."

She sighed. "I guess it isn't smart. Okay. Give me your key, dear. Where shall I meet you?"

"I'll hang around here."

She took the key. "It won't take me five minutes." She winked at him. "Coward!"

"I warned you."

He sat in a lobby chair. He waited five minutes, ten minutes, fifteen minutes. After twenty minutes had passed, he went up to his room. He rapped on the door. It opened a small cautious way, and then swung wide.

She walked away from him to stand by the terrace door, her back to the room.

He closed the room door and said, "Uh . . . get your film changed?"

"Yes, thank you," she said in a small rusty voice.

"Well . . . I wondered what was keeping you."

"I was just going to come back down. I took . . . some time out for tears."

He walked close to her, put his hands on her shoulders. "Tears?"

She shrugged his hands off and moved a step away. "For no good reason, I guess."

"Come on, Cory. What's the matter?"

She whirled and stared angrily at him. "Why do we have to be so damn scrupulous and decent? Who knows what's going to happen to anybody in the world tomorrow? Why do I have to be cheated? I've been cheated out of too much in my life." Her face twisted. "So I'm shameless. I want to go to bed with you. Please, please, please." She hurled herself at him, and he held her trembling body. With her face against his throat, she said, "Would it just be so terribly cheap it would spoil everything? Is it too soon?"

For an instant a ridiculous image came into his mind, a fragment of an old movie comedy, a man on the rickety wing of a high-flying airplane carefully pinching his nose before leaping wildly into space.

"Not cheap," he said. "And not soon."

"Yes," she said. "Yes," and looked at him gravely, intently, stepped to the drapery cords, yanking the pumpkin draperies closed to fill the room with orange light, like a room at the edge of some giant furnace.

When he saw her nude, there was a virginal economy about her figure, but all smoothly sheathed, all projection of bone muted, sleekly functional as a seal. The feel of her when she slid into his arms made him gasp for breath. The texture of her was dry, smooth, firm and curiously heated, like silk fresh from the iron.

When he awoke it was dark, and the tall ceramic lamp on the table between the beds was on. He awoke with no memory of having gone to sleep, and no memory of when the lamp had been turned on, or who had done it. He looked at his watch and saw that it was a quarter to nine. He was on his back, and felt as if the whole area from his heart to his knees had been hollowed out, leaving only a papery husk which would collapse if he moved without caution.

She sprawled asleep on the neighbor bed, prone, her face toward him in the lamplight, breathing deeply and slowly through the slack swollen lips. Her delicate face had a puffed, strained, misused look, a residue of fevers. In the thickets of recent memory he saw that face, moving in the pumpkin light now gone, at all angles and distances, always with the same look, glazed, deadened, intent, the eyes half closed, the mouth wider. And he heard the sounds, the nasal petulant whining when all was not just as she wanted it, and the rhythmic coughing gasps when things went well for her.

His mind drifted, forlorn, trying to find analogies which could help him perceive the relationship and understand what had happened. He felt that sense of loss one has when someone dear has died, and in a little while he understood he mourned the loss of Cory, the fictitious Cory of the sea breeze and the phone call. He missed a girl named Cory, forever gone.

You would feel this way, he thought, if you killed some kind of innocent thing with your hands. If you conspired to kill it. If the two of you pursued it in its terror for a long way over rough country, enduring your own exhaustion in the dark joy of the chase, and then caught it at last, tortured it for a long time, then bled it and gutted it and buried it and stomped the ground flat. It would be like this. You would not want to look directly at each other. You would be filled with a listless shame, but in some curious way you would be joined in a conspiracy of guilt. The worst of it, perhaps, is the knowledge that you will want to run the wild chase again.

Or, he thought, is it my own innocence I mourn? How could I have not known of this dimension in the world I'm in, where everything can be erased, leaving only the animal agony, the animal greed?

He turned his head to look at her again, and as he did so she opened her eyes. The light glinted on the tiny gold buttons in the small gentle ear lobes. Her eyes were an unfocused blue, and he saw them change as they saw him, saw them close and open again.

She pushed herself up, swung her legs off the bed to sit facing him. She gave an aching yawn, shuddered, scratched her head. "W'time is it?"

"Nearly nine," he said. "When did we go to sleep?"

"Donno, dear. It was dark." She stood up and swayed, then padded off into the bathroom. In a little while he heard the sound of the shower. He drowsed off and awakened when she touched his foot. She was sitting on the foot of his bed, looking at him. She looked at him with a mild, skeptical interest, the way a woman looks at something she might buy, if she can think of a use for it.

"You don't like me very much, do you?" she said.

"Let's just say I'm not delighted with myself, either."

She pulled her legs up, hugged them, her chin on her knees, looking at him with mockery. "Oh, you'll be delighted with yourself soon enough, Hubbard. You'll remember. You'll strut. You'll love telling your friends about it. You're a strong man, you know."

"What are you trying to prove, Cory?"

She tilted her head, and her eyes changed. For the first time he had the odd feeling that she was not entirely sane. "I've proved it, haven't I? I'm the best you ever had. I'm the best you'll ever have. I made you holler, and that was a brand new thing for you, wasn't it? Not like the other times you've done a little cheating, was it? Tell me I'm the best!"

"It's the first time I've cheated."

Her laugh was derisive. "Oh, come now!"

"It's the truth, Cory. Why would I lie to you?"

She looked uncertain, slightly troubled. "You're unusual, then. Why not?"

"Let's put it this way. I haven't really felt any need for anything I couldn't get with Jan. I've been curious about a few other women, but not enough to make it worth while loading myself with a lot of middle-class guilt."

"Now you've got something to feel guilty about, lover."

"It's going to take a while to sort out just how I'm going to feel about it."

Her smile was like a sneer. "I'll tell you one way you'll feel, darling. From now on, your darling, adorable, innocent Jan is going to be like so much oatmeal. Every time you have oatmeal, you'll remember steak."

"I don't think it will be that way, Cory. And I don't know why you should want it to be that way. You act right now as if you hate me. I think it's going to be fine with Jan and me, as it always has been."

"You'll find out."

"I'm not going to be comparing. This was something else."

"It was just exactly the same thing, dear, but better, because I'm better."

"I'll say you're not the way I thought you'd be."

"All girly-girl?" she said contemptuously. "Shy and blushing and sighing?"

"Something like that, yes."

"The film I was using. It says not to change film in bright sunlight, Floyd. That's all."

"And there was no time out for tears?"

"Of course not."

"Why the production, then?"

"I wanted you, and I didn't want to take the chance of scaring you off, darling. You like to pretend you're a decent man. I think that's very quaint and nice, really. And in the beginning, you were so cute and boyish, trying to be so manly, dear."

"I sort of lost the initiative pretty early in the game."

"You wouldn't have done much with it if I'd let you keep it. I knew you were irritated about that. I could tell. You were resisting me in little ways for quite a long time. And then you got to the point where you could stop thinking and worrying, and then I could give us a lot of hours of it."

A sudden anger tightened his throat. "I think you're an evil little bitch, Cory."

She laughed at him. "I'm a choosy evil bitch and a delicious evil bitch and a very competent evil bitch. And all this competence is all yours, dear, for the whole convention."

"No thanks."

She laughed again. "Try to say that tomorrow, when you start wondering if the things you think happened really happened. You'll want to find out all over again. You'll have to find out, Floyd. You're hooked, darling. Don't fight it. Why spoil the fun? My God, the way you look at me! Your little puritan soul is outraged. You hate me right now because I destroyed all your manly dignity and turned you into a rather untidy animal, and it hurts your pride to think how much there was that I had to teach you. By tomorrow, lover, you'll realize that I wasn't *using* you, and laughing at you. You'll remember that I was far too busy being my own kind of animal, and you'll remember how you learned to drive me practically out of my mind, and you'll feel so terribly masculine and eager, you won't be able to wait to get us in here with the door locked. Right now, lover, you're ruined. You'd get as much kick out of looking at a mailbox as you get out of staring at me. If I hugged you, you'd probably gag. It astonishes you that I ever looked good to you. But you just wait, brother. Just wait and see."

She got off the bed and began to get dressed, humming to herself. He could see movement out of the corner of his eye, but he did not watch her directly.

She came over and stood by the bed and said, "I'm off, darling."

"Cory?"

"Yes, dear."

"Why does it have to be so . . . antagonistic? Okay, you're not what you seemed to be. And you're something I never ran into before. And I'll admit I was overmatched. But why does it have to be like . . . some kind of revenge? I haven't tried to hurt you."

"You've hurt Jan, haven't you?"

"Possibly. What's that to you?"

"Absolutely nothing."

"Who are you getting even with?"

"Who's asking you to try to understand me, dear? Just enjoy me."

"You're uneasy. Why should my asking you that make you uncomfortable?"

"I'm terribly comfortable. I can think of a dozen lovely reasons why I'm at peace with the world, dear." She bent and kissed him lightly on the mouth. "Do get a *good* sleep. You'll need it."

He heard the door open and shut quietly behind her. In a little while he got up and took a long shower, soaping himself many times. After he had dressed, he looked at the convention program to see what he had missed.

Though the dinner speakers had not talked about any of his particular areas of interest, he vowed to miss no more of the scheduled events. He had also missed an official cocktail party prior to the banquet.

Hubbard felt curiously furtive as he rode down in the elevator. Noisy delegates got on at nearly every floor. He had the feeling that if anyone stared closely at him they could not fail to see the stains of strenuous debauch.

He ate alone at a small table in a small dining room of the hotel specializing in broiled meat. The flames under a large open broiler made a flickering light. He felt as if all reality had been distorted in some small prismatic way, just enough to make him feel wary and dubious. His hands did not look or feel like his own. The morsels of steak were alternately tasteless and delicious. He had the compulsion of all rational men to analyze, to reason, to reach conclusions—but his mind rebelled at all formal patterns. It veered, swooped, tilted—shying away from all structured devisings. He was tired and hungry and he did not want to think about Cory Barlund.

As he ate he became aware of another time in his life, long ago, when he had felt this same way, when he had experienced this same dull complexity of guilt, deceit and confusion. It took him many minutes to remember the exact incident, because he had buried it deeply, had camouflaged the placed where it lay with all the devices of self-esteem.

He had been twelve years old, a tough and resolute kid, hardened in urban ways, familiar with all the survival devices a large family must use when an industrial accident has permanently maimed the father, and the compensation is a little less than adequate. He knew the protocol of the gangs and the schoolyards, the uses of valor and guile. But a duality had come into his life at that time, a troublesome thing. He had been unable to completely conceal from his teachers his quickness of mind, and the quality of his imagination. No matter how carefully he cultivated the moronic expression, the monosyllabic answer, his grades were better than he wanted them to be. And he found himself saddled with a lust for reading. Reading was particularly reprehensible in his circles, outside the family, and he had to fill his need in complete secrecy. A slightly older boy named Mark learned of Floyd's secret vice. Mark was unacceptable. He was tall and plump. He could not run or fight or play games. He used big words, had a talent for sarcasm and responded to persecution by winding his arms around his head and squalling.

But Mark read books, and he steered Floyd toward some wonderful ones, and they would argue about what they had read. Mark also brought Floyd into a little group headed by Mr. Ellinder, an instructor in the high school, a man with a small mustache, a collection of pipes, and many shocking opinions about a lot of things Floyd had always taken for granted. They called the little group The Book League, and they had their meetings in the room over the garage where Mr. Ellinder lived with his mother and an aunt.

In that way the duality was partially resolved. Floyd could run with the pack, pretend dullness and indifference in school, and still have an outlet for expressions of the growing agility of his mind. He knew Mr. Ellinder was a great man who would be recognized by the world after his book was published. He had been working on it for a long time.

One rainy Saturday afternoon Floyd finished a book sooner than he had expected. Mr. Ellinder had loaned it to him. He wanted another book by the same man from Mr. Ellinder's library in the room over the garage. Mr. Ellinder had promised to lend it to him next. So he walked a dozen blocks with the book tucked carefully under his raincoat. He knocked at the garage door and there was no answer. He tried the door and it was unlocked. He went in furtively and moved silently up the narrow stairs, telling himself there would be no harm in leaving the book and taking the other one, because it had already been promised to him.

He had tiptoed halfway across the upstairs room toward the bookshelves when he heard a sound to his right. He snapped his head around and stared toward the dormer alcove where stood the old couch with the Navajo blanket on it, saw Mark there, looking soft and blurred and blind without his glasses, and saw, glaring at him over Mark's bare chubby shoulder, the fierce, indignant face of Mr. Ellinder.

"Get out!" Mr. Ellinder whispered. "Get out of here!"

Floyd had run all the way home through the rain. He lay on his bed and listened to the rain on the roof and tried not to think about anything. Mark arrived over an hour later. The rain had stopped. His mother called to him to tell him. Floyd did not ask Mark in. He went out into the small back yard.

"Paul wants to talk to you," Mark said with a nervous defiance.

"Paul?"

"Mr. Ellinder. He's scared you'll tell. He wants to talk to you."

Floyd had sobbed once, and hit Mark in the mouth as hard as he could, without warning. Mark sat down hard in the mud and began to cry like a girl. Floyd ran into the house and looked out the window and saw Mark get up and fumble around and find his glasses, wipe them on his shirt, put them on and walk away.

When he was back in his room, the room he shared with an older brother, Floyd felt very much the same way he now felt, as he finished the expensive meal in the resort hotel. Drained, dulled, guilty, mourning the loss of something which had never existed, yet half convinced he had been the agent of its destruction.

Seven

ON the morning of the second full day of the convention, Hubbard was up early. When he awakened, the pumpkiny orange glow in his room made him feel a sick, breathless excitement which he forced out of his mind as quickly as possible. He told himself he would be brisk, purposeful, cold and observant. As he ate breakfast, he studied the supplementary program of workshops and clinics and selected, as being potentially most useful to him, a discussion of foreign distribution methods and problems.

He was through breakfast twenty minutes before the discussion was scheduled to start, and so he checked the desk and found an unexpectedly thick airmail letter from Jan. He thumbed it open to see if there was any enclosure, but found only the sheets she had typed on her old portable.

"Darling, The kids are in bed and the idiot box is blessedly silent and all the emergencies of the day have been coped with, I think . . ."

He put it back in the envelope and put the envelope in his inside jacket pocket. He had a sudden feeling of disloyalty, so strong that he felt his face grow hot. The slight bulk of the letter in his pocket was an accusatory weight.

He walked along the exhibit ramp and noticed that the AGM twins were not yet on duty. A few people, moving slowly, were tidying their displays, putting out fresh stacks of brochures.' They were turning on the prism lights, the floodlights and the hooded fluorescents.

Hubbard found the far corner of the Convention Hall where the discussion would take place. Chairs were arranged in a semicircle facing the table where the panel would sit. Three men sat at the end of one aisle, talking quietly and intently. He took Jan's letter out and began to read it where he had left off.

"I am trying to think clearly, darling, and I want to put down exactly what I mean, so there will be no chance for you to misunderstand me. We seem to have a lot of trouble with misunderstanding lately. I guess I am taking the chance of trying to clear the air. Somebody has to. We have to talk to each other when you get back here and both make an effort to really communicate. What I am trying to do is give us a start on it. I am trying to give you something you can read and re-read and think about, in terms of us. I have been bitchy lately, and maybe my reasons aren't good, but at least I should be able to put them down calmly.

"I guess the simplest way to say it, darling, is to tell you that this isn't the cruise I signed up for. I can adjust myself to this kind of cruise, but first I have to be sure there's no way back to what I thought it would be.

"I hope it doesn't sound too corny to tell you that I know I married a dedicated man. I knew that you were concerned about the advancement of human knowledge in one small area where you are an expert. I knew you were willing to teach so you'd have the opportunity to do research. I was always joyous at your enthusiasms, darling. I did not expect we would ever have very much money. I expected you to work terrible hours and forget to eat and be so distracted by your work I would have to get used to wondering whether you remembered my name.

"It was like that, dear, exactly like that, and when it was like that we were both happier than we are now. We have a lot more money now. But things are not right, the way they used to be right. The last time I tried to tell you how I feel, it turned into the kind of argument we couldn't have had before our lives changed. You accused me of being discontented because you have to take so many trips. I do not like having you away at any time, but that is a secondary thing. Floyd, you made what you are doing sound very plausible, so plausible that I wonder if you believe it yourself. You made it a lot more intricate than this, but you told me, in effect, that if a man has a talent for administration, then he is not pulling his share of the load if he turns his back on it and restricts himself to technical things. You said that there are thousands of technicians and very few administrators, and without the ability of the administrators, the technicians would never get constructive things done. You said I was trying to hold you back, which was really a nasty and unfair thing for you to say.

"Darling, I don't want to try to argue about the validity of how a man should spend his life. You can argue that nothing can be proved valid, or argue that everything has its own validity. I am talking about *you*, about Floyd Hubbard. I cannot help it, darling, but this business of exalting the administrative stuff seems to me to be awfully tricky.

"Remember when you and Tony were running that long experiment on the conductivity of special alloys at absolute zero? I said to you, joking, 'When you do come up with something special, they'll use it to make better pots and pans.' Can you remember how legitimately angry you got with me? Can you remember the arguments you used? You were a man doing a man's work, and you were not afraid of idealism.

"Forgive me, but this administration thing you are in and have been in for at least two years seems to me to be the manipulation of human beings. Granted that you rearrange groups of people so they are more effective, and possibly happier, but it is nothing you can be particularly idealistic about.

"You have a thirst for knowledge, darling, and you seem to satisfy it best with tangible things. Now that you are dealing with these intangibles, you are changing. I do not know how to say it without hurting you or angering you, so all I can say is that you are losing a kind of innocence which was always dear to me. I think you take the wrong kind of pride in what you are doing. You are learning how to push the little buttons which make people jump, and you are becoming cynical and skeptical about people. It is a kind of 'watchfulness' which I see in you. Your smile is the same and you seem to talk in the same way, and people like you as readily as ever, but you are on guard, even with me. I think you are becoming a political man, and once again I must sound childish to you as I say that I do not like the by-products—the compromise, subterfuge and, so help me, the 'use' of human beings. Darling, I am not accusing you of some enormous wickedness. But I think the kind of work you are doing now will change the essential texture of you, will harden you in ways I cannot clearly understand.

"I can understand though how tempting it all is to you. You have a power you never had before, and you can tell yourself that you are using that power on the side of the angels. You can also tell yourself that you are finding a wonderful security for your family.

"Though I am writing all this, I am still not such a fool as to ask you to give it up, to demand of you that you go back to the kind of work I thought you would always do. All I am asking, humbly, is that you think about all these things, and examine yourself to see how happy you are. If we are not happy, all the rest is not worth it. I am not a very complicated woman. I love you, and I want you to love me, and I think love is easier all around when life has good meanings, when work is good, and there are tangible ways to measure what you accomplish.

"I am asking you to think about it and when you come back to me, be ready to talk about it to me in such a way that we will not start trying to wound each other with words, just because both of us, perhaps, feel a little bit guilty. I can promise you that if you are convinced this is what you want to do with your life, I can certainly go along with it and do the best I know how. We have had a good thing working for us for a long time, darling, and I would crawl through glass, fire and cactus to keep it, and I think you would too. This good marriage is the product of luck, skill and labor. I just want to be terribly sure that we do not needlessly handicap ourselves. Do you understand? It sounds very spoiled and surly for me to say this is not the cruise I signed up for. Maybe nobody gets—or is entitled to get—exactly what they bargained for. But I can make a try, can't I?

"Please don't phone me about this, dear. It will be better to talk it all out face to face. So, while you are conventioneering about and doing this dirty little job for John Camplin, keep me in mind from time to time and try to get outside yourself and look back in and see if there's been any changes made, any that you don't especially like. I do love you. Jan."

As he put the letter back in his pocket he looked up and saw the panel members were in place. About twenty-five men occupied chairs in the area that would have seated five times that number.

The moderator said, "I hoped that more members of this joint convention would have recognized the importance of the area we are discussing this morning. I can only tell the men sitting up here with me that I hope others will join us during the course of the morning, and I am ashamed at predicting such an optimistic turnout."

As the moderator began the introductions of the members of his panel, a lean balding man on Hubbard's right turned and said in a low voice, "Lou should know better by now, for God's sake. Most of them are hung over and sacked out. Some are out by the pool getting their health back. The golf tournament is this afternoon. I know a couple marathon poker games going on. Some groups went out deep sea fishing. Lou is lucky there's this many." He glanced at Hubbard's badge. "AGM, hey? Jesse Mulaney's boys. Where you located?"

"Houston."

"Jud Ewing, Federated—outa Chicago." They shook hands. "I've known Jesse a lot of years. Be seeing you at the AGM cabana this afternoon, I suppose."

"Yes. Yes, of course," Hubbard said.

He tried to keep his mind on the discussion. He kept losing the thread of the arguments. He stuck it out for a little over an hour, until the moderator decreed a five minute break, and then he quietly walked away. As he started to walk past the AGM exhibit, he saw Fred Frick inside the enclosure talking to one of the twins. The other twin sat on an aluminum chair, working on her fingernails. Fred was grinning, grimacing, bobbing his head as he talked to the girl. Hubbard noticed that the girl's expression was placid, slightly surly, unimpressed and uninvolved.

"Floyd! Hey, Floyd!" Fred called. Hubbard turned and went over to the exhibit. Fred and the twin moved closer to the velvet rope. "Floyd, I want you should meet Honey. Honey, this is Mister Floyd Hubbard, one of the brilliant young executives of AGM out of the home office in Houston, Texas."

"Please to meetchew," she said with colossal indifference.

"The girls have dresses on today. I guess you prolly noticed," Frick said and jabbed Hubbard in the ribs with his thumb. "Mulaney figured it would be a little more dignified."

dive into the pool, check it with your foot first, to see if it's the pool. We don't want people diving into mirages."

He thanked Bobby and took another quick look around, looking for Cory. He did not quite dare ask about her. He thought he could make it casual enough, but he was not quite certain.

When he turned to stretch out, he saw her standing six feet beyond his sun cot, standing and smiling at him, and he had no way of telling how long she had been there. She had a bathing cap in her hand. She wore a two-piece swim suit in a bold diagonal pattern of oyster and coral. It was wet, and droplets of water stood on her shoulders.

The first look at her was like having an electric current run through his body. He had not realized to what extent he had been sensitized to her. "Got to get my towel and stuff," she said, and walked by the cot. He watched her walk away from him. It seemed grotesque to him that she should look and walk like a lady. It seemed like some confusing miscarriage of justice that she could walk in front of all the world and seem fragile in her loveliness, tender and tidy and poised. There should have been a vulgar pouting of those merciless hips, an obscene slant to that tormenting mouth, some suggestion in her walk of that rubbery suppleness of body, that limber wildness, she used in such an inventive abandon that no dimension of her, no texture or convolution of her was forgotten to a rhythmic using. Yet here she was, untouched and untouchable, a very pretty slender girl with toffee hair and dark-blue blue eyes, and a sweet and delicate sculpturing of face.

He lay back and closed his eyes against the sun glare that came through his dark glasses, and felt the sweat begin to exude from his pores.

There was a round touch against his leg just above his ankle, and the effect was as if she had run her fingernails lightly up the inside surface of his leg and nested her fist in his groin. "Hi," she said.

He opened his eyes and saw that she sat on the foot of the sun cot, and had pulled her feet up and was hugging her legs. Her chin rested on her knees. It was the same posture he had seen her in at the foot of his bed, naked from her shower, and he knew it was intentional. And she knew what it was doing to him.

"I . . . have to take back some kind of a tan to prove I was here," he said in a weak attempt at casual conversation. He knew he had made an error in not moving into the middle of one of the small groups.

"I don't like to stay in the sun too long in a suit," she said. "It spoils my tan. Did you notice, dear, yesterday? I'm tan all over."

"Not so loud!"

"Nobody can hear us, darling. Did you sleep well? Did you dream about me?"

"Let's try a new topic, Cory."

"Last night I'd almost decided to stay right there with you, and then I remembered I hadn't fed Maynard. He's my cat, a truly enormous demanding beast, half Siamese, half alley. As opposed to me, dear. I'm all alley, as I hope you noticed."

"Cory!"

"I gorged him before I left, and left him another enormous bowl of goodies, so I can stay with you tonight, Floyd darling, free of the weight of responsibility."

"Now listen . . ."

"So, whenever you're ready, and you feel strong, we'll just stroll away from here, one by one."

"No, Cory."

"You don't want me?"

"That isn't the point. It's just that . . ."

"I want you, and that's what matters isn't it? You'd be terribly flattered if you knew how unusual that is, dear. The few times I ever do want anyone, I never want them again. But I could eat you alive. Believe me, darling, I can take it or leave it, and usually it's a case of going through the motions."

"Can I get you a drink?"

"Bobby is bringing me one, thanks. As I was saying, you should be flattered. What's so great about you, anyway? You're kind of a stumpy little man, and you look as if you might drive a cab for a living, and you have sad, melting brown eyes, and you don't have any special talent for making love, and I have shocked the hell out of you. What is it about you, dear?"

She stopped as Bobby brought her a drink. She thanked

him and said, "I'm delving into the motivations of an AGM executive type now."

"They're the tricky ones," Bobby said.

"Really, Bobby, your Mr. Hubbard seems to have very conventional ideas."

"I'm at a convention, no?" Floyd said.

Bobby groaned and Cory said, "That isn't the sort of conventional ideas I meant, sir." Somebody called Bobby and he excused himself and walked away.

"Where were we, dear?" Cory asked.

"We were nowhere."

"Do you think so? After all my hard labor?" She placed her hand on his ankle and began to stroke him almost imperceptibly. "I have to see just how invulnerable you are, darling."

He fixed his mind on remote things which might save him. A winter waterfall. The pass patterns of the Baltimore Colts. The time he had the automobile accident. But the pressure, gentle, insistent, moved into each thought and moved it aside.

"If you try to be too stubborn, little bull, you'll disgrace us all," she said in a singsong tone. He hitched sideways abruptly, and rolled over into his face. She laughed softly and no longer touched him.

"So invulnerable," she said. "Such a total rejection of poor Cory."

She got up and came around and sat crosslegged on the concrete, facing him. "Why do you feel as if you have to fight it?"

"Because there are so many reasons why I shouldn't bother. Can you understand that? All the rational reasons. Why lock the barn doors, and so forth. And who has to know? And when will you ever get a chance at anything like this again? Pat reasons, Cory. But every one of them cheapens me and diminishes me."

"Why you? I took the initiative. I'm taking it again."

"That's the most insidious reason of all."

She looked slightly startled. Her eyes seemed to change, to become more sober and thoughtful. "Maybe you're as new a something to me as I am to you."

"Maybe."

"You seemed to like it, Floyd."

"That's a pretty pale word. I got a terrible dirty joy out of it. It was more like a battle. It wasn't love. Love

isn't like that. We were antagonists. Like wrestling
snakes and wondering how many bites you can endure
before the venom kills you You were full of contempt,
Cory. You were trying to punish both of us."

"Of course."

"Then you realize that?"

"Who claims it isn't a battle? Only a novice would
think it isn't."

"You're no novice."

"I told you I was married once."

"I don't mean that."

As she studied him he looked at her mouth in sunlight, at the almost invisible down on her upper lip, at
the firm modeling of those lips, and found it almost impossible to relate the harmless image to that remembered
agony the flickering tongue could produce, to the schooled
cruelty of lips and teeth, to the thready whimperings
and gutteral gaspings and the petulant, incredible de-
mands.

"Do I make you sick?" she whispered.

"Yes."

"Good! I'll make you sicker and stronger. You're a
silly little man, you know. Silly and helpless and terribly
shocked. I'm making love to you right now in my mind
I'm thinking of things you couldn't believe. They're boil-
ing around in my mind. My breasts are starting to hurt,
lover. And my   ."

"Stop it, Cory! Please stop it!"

"The more you can hate me, the better it will be."

"Cory, I'm not going up there with you. I mean it.
It happened, and I suppose I'm even grateful in some
eerie way, but I'm also smart enough to know this could
. . . so easily turn into a compulsion. And that's what I
think you really want. You want me to lose the last fragment of myself, and be . . . be turned into a swine."

"What made you say that? What made you use that
word?"

"Why are you so agitated? It seems apt enough. As
soon as I start ignoring everything in the world but you,
and what you can do to me, then you'll walk away."

"But wouldn't it be worth it?"

"Not to me, Cory. Not to me. I have a horrible afflic-
tion. Pride. And I'm trying to keep my own good opin-

ion of myself. And I want no more of you.   Thanks a lot."

"Big talk. Big brave puritanical talk. I'll be in your bed soon enough. And you'll be happy about it. Wait and see. Let me know when you're ready. Because I've been ready, terribly ready, ever since I woke up this morning, lover."

She rose easily to her feet, traced the line of his jaw with her fingertips and walked away, pausing to sip her drink and look back at him, mocking him. She turned slightly toward him and made such a small, quick, imperceptible movement of her hips that he knew no one else could have noticed it, but to him it was like taking a skilled boxer's blow directly under the heart. It stopped his breath and chilled his limbs. She went over to where Charlie Gromer and Tom Carmer were watching Stu Gallard whipping Fred Frick at gin rummy. He closed his eyes. The heat and light seemed to hold him suspended in a lazy void where his mind moved in a gluey rhythm and nothing was particularly important. His mind swung back to Cory, to visual memories of her which, in his sun-struck state, had the power of hallucination—a breast so close to his eyes in pumpkin light it blotted out two thirds of the world, a tidy, perfect breast, firm as papaya, with the tan-orange texture of the nipple area pulled shiny-tight in erectile joy—the milky musky texture of the skin at the back of her knee against his lips—and, stretching away from him, the slender V of her back, topped at a distance remote as in delirium by the toffee tangle of her hair, while her clenched hips burst upon his lap, as impossible to capture, as muscularly tantalizing as the fresh caught fish that leaps its life away on the floorboards of the boat. . . .

He knew he had slept, and was surprised that he had. The sun had moved through a long segment of its arc. Most of them were gone. Cory was gone. He thought of her and felt the heavy weakness of the convalescent. The fever had broken for a time. He walked to the pool and swam four slow lengths. There was a bad taste in his mouth, and his arms and legs felt leaden.

He walked back and was standing, toweling himself, by the sun cot when Connie Mulaney came over, a tall rum drink in each hand. "If you say no, Floyd, I'll have

to drink them both, and I'll make a spectacle of myself."
He took the drink, realizing she was holding herself
under careful control, that she was considerably drunker
than she looked.

She sat on the cot and patted the place beside her and
said, "I want to get to know you before this whole damn
thing is over, dear."

He sat down and she touched glasses clumsily and
said, "Here's to sin."

"To sin."

"Everybody going. Host and hostess stuck till the
dirty end. Look at my Jesse over there, snowing Jud
Ewing. Both telling brave lies to each other. You know
what?"

"What, Connie?"

"If this time you'd called me Mrs. Mulaney, I'd give
you a hit right in the head. You got an instinct for those
things, haven't you?"

"For what?"

"For what to call people to get the right effect."

"Do I seem to plan everything that carefully?"

"No, dear. You do it cute. I'm old enough to be your
mother. You know that?"

"That's a lie!"

"Not if I was from Kentucky, believe me. I don't know
if I'd want a son like you. It would scare me, a little."

"Why would it scare you?"

"You've got all your ducks in a row. That's an old
expression."

"It may look it to you, Connie, but believe me, my
ducks are scattered around every which way."

She peered at him. "What'd I want to say to you anyhow?"

"I guess you're telling me I'm tricky."

Her white hair looked slightly unkempt. The drinks
had sagged her face. "Y'know, dear, there's a new kind of
people in the world," she said. "Can't understand them.
Smooth quiet people. Exactly so many drinks. Right
clothes and right car and right opinions. Don't you get
bored with yourself?"

"Doesn't everybody, Connie?"

"Me? Four kids married, three grandbabies. I don't
get bored with me. Or Jesse." She leaned closer and
looked at him with a slurred challenge. "You know I

still like to go to bed with him? You young ones, you
think there's something nasty about that, don't you?" She
patted her stomach. "Stayed nice for him. As nice as I
could. You know what it is, dear? It's . . . it's a giving
sweetness. It's cozy. It's like saying all the years are
right. Will you have that, when you're an old hulk like
my Jesse?"

"I hope so."

"I'm still his best girl. That's a good thing . . . isn't it?"

"It's a good thing, Connie."

"Ah, how well I know him, Floyd! How well! He wants
to be a tricky son of a bitch. He wants to be cute too.
But it doesn't work for him. He's trying something now.
Do you know that? I do. I don't know what it is, but
he feels guilty about it. It could have something to do
with you. He's scared of you, dear. We both are. You're
one of the new kind of people."

"I don't want you to feel like that."

"You watch out for my Jesse. What was I saying to
you? There was something I wanted to . . . oh, it's
him and Jud telling lies to each other as if everything was
all right. I love him. I told you that, didn't I? But he
has to keep tearing himself apart, because no one will
tell him. I shouldn't talk to you. But it's in your hands,
isn't it? You could be my son, and it's in your hands
and nobody knows what you're thinking. I shouldn't say
these things to you. I'm an old drunken woman, and I
don't know how to handle the new people. I say the
wrong things. Hell with it. So I can say the wrong things
to you. What'll happen to my Jesse?"

"I don't know, Connie."

She looked at him with a great intensity. "What'll you
say should happen? The new kind of people never tell
you anything. It all comes out later on punch cards.
You got the guts to tell me?"

He looked out across the ramps and terraces, the
pools and plantings. The sun was low, and the slant of
its golden light accentuated the tan of the few who were
left, the last ones who were leaving. The pale flanks of the
hotel structures rose toward the graying sky. His heart
felt like a stone, but somewhere within him was a pride
without mercy.

"I don't know what they'll do," he said, making himself
look directly into her eyes. "But I'll report what I

believe. That's what I'm paid for. I'll say that due to the
seniority policies of AGM, he got about three big steps
higher than he could have gone on merit. I'll say the job
he holds is so far beyond his capacities, he makes wild
swings in the dark. I'll say that the whole structure, per-
sonnel, policy, recruiting, control methods, needs a complete revamp, and it will be facilitated by getting him
entirely out of the picture as soon as possible."

She looked at him and tried to speak, moistened her
lips and tried again. "I . . . I've known that. He has too,
I think." She brought her hands up to her face and
sat with her chin lowered.

"He won't be told that way," Hubbard said.

"Did I have to be told that way?"

"Maybe I was wrong, Connie."

She dropped her hands and snuffled once. "Oh, you
couldn't be wrong, dear! You new people are always
right. There's always a reason. It's never evident in the
beginning." Her face twisted. "You know what I miss?
Kindness. There used to be a lot of it around. When
there weren't any reasons for it, I guess. But now
it's a different kind of thing. You don't want kindness
from somebody who won't bring their own troubles to
you. Because if it goes just one way, it's like pity. It's
like social workers or something. We've got to find our
way through a maze, and you people look down through
the glass and turn the current off and on to sting our
feet, and you smile at us when we come out right."

"Connie, it isn't like that."

She gave him a smile almost of triumph. "But that's the
way it *feels*, dear. To us. So what the hell difference
does it make how it feels to you? There's a chart someplace where you can look Jesse up, and there's a footnote
to turn to page seventy-eight, paragraph four, and there
I am. You see, dear, if it kills him, there's nothing I
can do to you. Nothing."

Jesse and Jud Ewing came strolling toward them, laughing at a joke. Jesse said, "Well, honey, we bombed them
all, and you too, it looks like, and the party is over.
What have you been bending Floyd's ear about?"

Hubbard felt sudden tension. "Oh, I've just been ram-
bling on and on, boring Floyd with stories of the old
days."

"It's been very interesting," Hubbard said.

"Well, let's all get prettied up, and we'll see you in the suite, Floyd. You drop in too, Jud."

Mr. and Mrs. Mulaney headed off toward the hotel.

Ewing said, surprisingly, "I was so damn bad off in love with her a whole damn lifetime ago."

"You were?"

"I worked for him in Nashville. I was single, and I used to get asked over for dinner. She was beautiful then, in that way they have when you can tell they're going to stay beautiful until the day they die. Without her, Jesse would still be making sleeper jumps and lugging a sample case. I married twice, pretending I was marrying her, but those things don't work out. And do you know something? This is the first time in thirty years I ever saw her get tight? Jesse always did enough drinking for two."

"She's a fine woman, Mr. Ewing."

Ewing gave him a long shrewd look. "But there comes a time when finally there just isn't any last string left on the bow. See you around, Mr. Hubbard."

Hubbard picked up his towel, lotion and sunglasses and followed slowly. Waiters moved through the dusk light, picking up glasses, moving furniture back where it belonged. A muscular boy was folding the trampolines and hooding them for the night. Sweeping crews were moving across the sun cot area. Other crews were vacuuming the pools. The outdoor bars were closing.

It was easy, Jan, he said to himself. Nothing to it. Like falling off a log. Like falling off the top of a sixty-foot log. Why, with the edge on my little hatchet, I could shave with it.

Eight

ROOMS 852 and 854 were interconnecting, but the door was closed and locked between them when Dave Daniels led Fred Frick into 852 and shut the door.

"Now we'll have a nifty little drink," Dave said.

"Damn it, Dave, I've been telling you, I got a lot of things to do. Unless I keep on top of things every minute . . ."

"Stop flapping around, for Chrissake! Here's your drink."

"I've had enough, and you've had enough," Frick said, taking the glass and sitting on the bed. "I've been meaning to talk to you, Dave, for your own good."

"Yes, father."

"Take it seriously, boy, because it is serious. You've got the Chicago setup, and you've done a good job, which I'll be the first to admit, but the way you're acting around here, you can bitch the whole thing. People are talking about it, Dave."

"Screw them all, every one."

"But you're not doing Jesse any good. Don't you have any loyalty? He's given you your break. Maybe you don't care what you do to yourself, but you're hurting Jesse in front of this Hubbard."

"Screw that little Greek too."

"Who says he's Greek?"

"He looks Greek. And you look like a Swede pimp. You know that, Freddy? Just like a Swede pimp."

Frick stood up. "You're too drunk to make any sense. I didn't come in here to . . ."

"Sit down or I'll sit you down!" Dave Daniels roared. His voice softened. "Okay. So maybe I've been a little bit out of line. I'm willing to admit it."

"So?" Frick said warily.

"What's got me so all messed up, old buddy, is that

little Barlund broad, and that's what I brought you in here about. She keeps brushing me off, and I want her so bad it makes my teeth ache. You're in charge of arrangements, Freddy, and this is one arrangement you're going to help me make, by God, or I'll spread pieces of those big yellow teeth of yours all over this goddam hotel."

"But . . ."

"I don't care how we work it, just as long as we work it. If I could just get her into this room and get ahold of her before she turns to run, I'll carry on from there, and she'll love every minute of it. But what you got to do, you got to think up some kind of story conference on this thing she's writing, and then . . ."

"You shouldn't get yourself so worked up about that little prostitu . . ."

"What was that, Freddy? What was that you said?"

"Just a manner of speaking, Dave. Honest. That's all."

Daniels stared at him. Frick looked uneasily at the bloodshot eyes, and at the long, heavy, leathery face and the brute hands. Daniels said, "That little girl wouldn't be a whore, now would she?"

"What's the matter with you, Dave? That's a silly question."

A big hand grabbed the front of Frick's suit, lifted him lightly off the bed, and ran him backwards into the far wall. He hit so hard it dazed him. Daniels' big face was inches from his. "You don't lie worth a damn, Frick. What do you know that I don't know?"

"Honest, Davie, there's nothing at all that . . ."

The big fist slammed him in the stomach. Frick fell onto his hands and knees and gagged helplessly. Daniels picked him up and stood him against the wall again.

"Are you nuts?" Frick shouted. "I'm not a well man. I got an ulcer. You could kill me doing that, you silly bastard!"

Daniels hit him again, picked him up again and held him against the wall. He grinned at Frick and said, "Honest to God, Freddy, I'm so drunk I don't know what I'm doing. I just might stand here and belt you until I'm worn out."

"Wait! Hey, wait!"

Daniels lowered his big fist. "Going to talk?"

"Okay. Yes. But let me sit down. Damn you! You ought to be locked up."

"You start kidding around, Freddy, and you get it again, maybe a little lower."

Fred Frick sat on the bed and made a grimace of pain. "You better not tell Jesse I told you. Cory is a call girl. We lined her up through an old friend of mine and Jesse's. She's as high class as anything you can find this side of New York. This story thing is a fake. We sicked her onto Hubbard."

"Onto Hubbard?"

"The idea being that she gets him to make an obvious damn fool of himself, and if he doesn't, she'll pull one hell of a scene in front of everybody that'll give him a different kind of reputation with AGM than the one he's got. Then he won't be so anxious to slip the knife to Jesse, and if he does, they're going to maybe take it with a grain of salt, because word will get back about how he got a little carried away at the convention."

"What makes you think that'll do any good?"

"What else is there to try?"

"Remember that auditor in St. Louis? They gave him a mickey and stripped him raw and turned him loose in the lobby, and it didn't do those boys at UFA a damn bit of good. All they got was a new auditor."

"Jesse thought it was worth a try."

"So Hubbard is getting it? I get near him and get a little kicking room, and he won't want any more of it for a long time."

"Now, dammit, Dave, you stay the hell out of this."

"Dave Daniels doesn't get brushed off by a whore."

"Dave, listen to me. This girl isn't any twenty-dollar trick. I know all about her. She's as choosy as if she was a debutante. She takes the business she wants to take and that's all. You knowing the score won't make any difference to . . ."

"Freddy old Frick, it's going to make a lot of difference, a hell of a lot of difference."

"Please, Dave, don't mess it up. You don't need her. Listen, fella, let me line you up something that'll make her look like . . ."

"No thanks."

"She's a scrawny kid, Dave."

Dave grinned at him. "Yeah. Isn't she though?"

"Don't mess me up with Jesse. And don't mess Jesse up. And there's another thing, Dave. If you give Hubbard a hard time, how long do you think you'll stay with AGM?"

"You're scaring me. I got a place I can go any time, for more money. In fact, pal, I'm sending in my resignation as soon as I get back. So what do I owe you, or that slob Jesse Mulaney, or that Hubbard shit?"

"I took a hell of a chance telling you all this, Dave."

"You would have taken a worse chance not telling me. You would have been carrying your guts in a hand basket, Freddy."

Frick got up hastily, moved out of Daniels' reach, and sidled to the door. "Just be reasonable," he begged.

Daniels laughed at him. "I know why you're in a big hurry. You want to find her and warn her. It won't do any good."

"You ought to be locked up. You go crazy when you drink."

Daniels faked a lunge toward him. Frick popped out into the corridor and slammed the door and ran a half dozen steps before slowing down. He wiped the palms of his hands on his handkerchief. With each deep breath he tried to take, his stomach hurt, and he felt slightly nauseated.

He stopped and leaned against the wall and wiped the sweat off his face. In a few minutes he was able to think more calmly and logically. He went to one of the bedrooms of the hospitality suite, found a number in his notebook and called it.

"Al, boy? Fred Frick. How's everything with you? That's good to hear. Al, I'm at a convention at the Sultana, and I've got a little problem maybe you can help me on. One of our crowd is heading for trouble. A nice guy, but he doesn't drink good, you know? So I want him taken out of the play before he can do himself some real harm. No, I think he might talk himself out of there too fast. He looks like he's handling it better than he is. I was thinking in terms of that ward at the hospital, and some shots to keep him quiet until . . . maybe Sunday? What's that? Oh, sure, you clear it with the hotel people. I understand. They don't want a fuss any more than I do. Dave Daniels, his name is. Chicago, Illinois. Al, one thing, he's a big son of a bitch. Yes. And use an ambulance? Sure. Do it any way you think best. Not until when? Al, I was hoping for a little faster service on this. It's seven-fifteen now. Well, I guess all we can do is keep our fingers crossed until ten. I'll make it a point to be right here in the suite at ten o'clock then. Eight sixty. You fellows come right on up. Yes, I'll take full responsibility. Dave will thank me when it's all over. Thanks loads, Al boy."

When Hubbard went into his room after coming from the cabana party, he was becoming increasingly curious about Cory Barlund. He could not quite believe she had given up. Dusk had brought shadows into the room. He turned the lights on. The maid had turned both beds down. He tossed the towel in a corner of the bathroom, pulled the swim trunks off, kicked the sandals off, and adjusted the shower to his liking. A few moments after he was under the hard spray, without any warning, slim arms clasped him around the waist. He made a reasonable attempt to jump out of his skin. "Guess who?" she called gayly.

He pried her clasped hands apart and turned toward her. She wore her swim cap, and it made her face look like the face of a young, sensitive boy. She looked implishly at him, snatched the soap from the tray and began to industriously lather his chest. He took the soap away from her. "How did you get in here?"

"I just opened the glass door, darling, and stepped in."

"How did you get into the room?"

"I asked the maid very politely, and gave her a tip, dear. Did I do something wrong? This is a convention, remember, and the rules are a little different. Oh, I've been here a long time. What kept you?"

"Where were you when I came in?"

"Skulking in the back of the closet. I ducked in there when I heard your key in the door. You see, dear, I thought you'd go right back into that stern and righteous routine and make everything as difficult as possible, so I thought this would save a hell of a lot of time, actually. Now you may scrub me sweetly and tenderly, and take me to bed."

"No, Cory."

She looked at him with a sly amusement. "No?"

He thrust her hand away. "Any other evidence is meaningless, Cory. The answer is no."

"Why are you wasting all this sterling character on a hopeless situation?"

He took her by the shoulders, turned her around, and thrust her out into the bathroom. "Go put something on."

"Yes, dear. Of course, dear. Anything you say, dear."

The only clothing he had brought into the bathroom were fresh shorts and socks. When he had them on, he went into the bedroom. She had left one lamp on. She had arranged herself with due care to lighting. "I'm trying to look like that Spanish postage stamp, lover. But I don't have the weapons she has. Come here."

He put on a white shirt and trousers. As he was buttoning the shirt he moved closer to the bed and looked at her without any expression.

"You do mean it, don't you?" she asked in quite a different voice, a small and rather wary voice.

"For a while the issue was in doubt. But not any more, Cory. You make it so damn difficult. I'm not trying to say I'm any better than you are. I'm not, for the love of God, saying you aren't desirable. And I couldn't ever say that this is an easy thing to do. But I can manage it. I'm fighting for survival, Cory. It's a strong instinct. If today became another yesterday, I think I'd be destroyed."

"Am I destroyed?"

"I don't know. In one sense, possibly. I don't know enough about you."

With a sudden smooth economy of movement she slid under the sheet and single blanket and covered herself to the chin.

"Please turn off the light, Floyd."

"But I'm telling you that it . . ."

"This is something else. Please. Then come and sit by me, and hold my hand."

"But . . ."

"It won't cost you anything to be kind, will it?"

He turned off the light. Some of the outside lighting made a faint glow on the ceiling. He took her hand when she reached toward him, and he sat on the bed.

"Maybe I can talk to you as a person, Floyd. I don't know."

"I like you, Cory. Does that help?"

"Yes. That helps. I was here alone for a long time. I read Jan's letter."

He took a deep breath and let it out. "You had no right, you know."

"I know. She seems very nice. She seems sweet and wise. Wives should be both, I guess, but not overly sweet, and not conspicuously wise. I tried to be that way with Ralph. I was quite good at it, too. Everyone seemed to think so. Even Ralph. I was an adorable little wife, Floyd. I had the constant image of myself being an adorable and adoring little wife, and I relished it. It was a game, I guess. Trying to do as well as the grownups. Do you know?"

"Yes, of course."

"Ralph was a properly boyish husband, with a good job. We agreed we'd have one year of just each other, and then start a baby. That's just what we did. The bed part was good, dear. Not like yesterday with us. Sweet and melting. All he had to do was reach out toward me, and my head would get so heavy I couldn't hold it up. I was very earnest about being everything he could ever want. He'd tell me I was all the women in the world. Isn't that sweet?"

"I guess it's supposed to be that way."

"When I was three months pregnant, he had to go to Havana on a business trip. When he came back, I gave him a loving welcome. Oh, very loving indeed. But the poor dear had picked up a little packet of syphilis from a Cuban whore. By the time there was a sore, he'd infected me. The doctor he went to called me up and had me come in. He was very jolly. It didn't have to be a tragedy. Not in this day and age. They'd knock it right out with massive doses of penicillin. But I got a bad reaction to the penicillin, and ran a high fever, and later they explained to me that it was the fever, not the infection, which turned my baby into an idiot. The third month is a bad time to have fevers, you know. So I was almost all women to my boyish husband. He needed a Cuban whore to fill out the ranks."

Her hand tightened convulsively on his, then became inert. The silence was long and clumsy.

"There isn't much to say, Cory. Bad luck? What can anybody say?"

"Oh, I think you need the rest of it before you make any comments. By the way, I'm a clean girl now. Don't be alarmed."

"You didn't have to say that, you know."

"I got the fastest divorce on record, dear. The baby is in a place in Maryland. It's over five years old now. It will never speak or walk or recognize anything or anyone. He pays the freight. Two fifty a month. That's the only settlement. They say they usually die in their early teens when they're like that. After the divorce I was trying in an amateur way to prove to every man in the world that I was more useful than every whore in Havana, until a domineering old slob of a woman named Alma Bender took me home and nursed me back into decent physical condition, and taught me the trade."

"The trade?"

"I'm on call, darling. All night stands only. A bill and a half, split ninety to me and sixty to Alma, because I maintain my own place. I'm twenty-eight years old, darling, and I average eight tricks a month, or a hundred a year, and I've had four fine years, and I think I can promise myself another ten or eleven. I take care of myself. Fifteen hundred men would be a nice memorable figure, don't you think? I'm choosy, you know. Want to know my stipulations?"

"Should I?"

"They have to be reasonably youngish, intelligent, fairly sensitive, married and . . . there should be a slight boyishness about them, just enough to remind me of Ralph. Then do you know what I do?"

"I think I have a clinical idea."

"No, darling. Beyond that. What I do is spoil them, so that they'll spend the rest of their lives knowing they'll never have it so good again. I clobber them so completely, they'll be forever wistful as they lie beside their little oatmeal wives and remember how it was."

"Revenge?"

"Of course. I'm their Havana whore. I'm the sword of justice. I give them the disease no drug can ever cure. I give them the ultimate experiences, lover, so that from that night on, nothing will ever completely satisfy them again. When they're moaning and shuddering and gibbering, I'm laughing inside. When they want to buy a woman, and they buy me, they never stop paying for it. Sometimes I let myself enjoy them Like with you. But almost always I fake. I put on a hell of a production, lover. It may even be better than the real thing. When it's real, I lose track a little."

"Do you tell all of them this?"

She pulled her hand away. "I've never told any of them this. All whores have hearts of gold. Haven't you heard? Haven't you met Suzie Wong? I enjoy my work, dear. I despise all you slobs, every one. Even you, lover. But you see, this is just a little different, because you didn't come waving your money. You're not technically the sort of customer I'm accustomed to."

"Technically? What the hell, Cory! What is this?"

"Oh, you're sort of the gift certificate type. I shouldn't tell you, but I don't expect it matters much one way or the other. You're the guest of Frick and Mulaney, dear. So enjoy. It's such a special deal, lasting so long, dear Alma clipped them for seven and a half, but only four hundred to me."

He stood up and paced to the terrace door. "But why?"

"Is that so hard? I'm going to make a big ugly public scene over you before this clambake is over. A horrid type named Amory has cautioned me to take it easy in the public rooms of the hotel when I go dramatic. You're going to be hung as a sheep so you'll ease off on Mr. Mulaney, obviously. And since you are going to be hung as a sheep anyway, dear, why don't you come to bed like a lamb?"

"Those silly bastards!"

"I probably talked too much. You're too easy to talk to, do you know that?"

"I've cultivated the talent." He sat beside her again. "On my word of honor, Cory, scene or no scene, I still give Mulaney the business. I've committed myself. Now the only thing such a scene could do is hurt me with the people I work for. So how about giving it up?"

"Don't be silly! I promised, and I was paid."

"But it won't do any good!"

"Lover, I couldn't care less."

"A heart of gold. Dear God!"

"You'll never, never forget me, Floyd. Every time you mount your darling Jan, I'll be riding your shoulders like a witch, jeering at you, boy."

"It won't be that way, believe me, but why the big boot out of punishing me? I didn't buy you. I was a damn fool, thinking I was irresistible."

"You cheated on your marriage, didn't you?"

"Yes, but it was . . ."

"So you get a little more than you asked for. And the fee is paid, lover. So you might as well get the use of it. So go walk around if you have to. Go have a drink or two. Think of me. I'll be right here in your bed, cozy and warm and ready, waiting for you."

"Why don't you get dressed and go home?"

"Why should I make it easy for you, you sanctimonious bastard? You're crawling with guilt and you think you can lighten the burden by refusing a second chance. You can't get clean that easy, not after yesterday. If the murderer lets his next victim walk away, does that turn him into a saint?"

"Maybe it's just that all of a sudden the merchandise looks shopworn."

"You tried the low blow, boy, and it doesn't work."

He dressed slowly. By the time he was finished, she was asleep. She had turned onto her side, and in the reflected light she looked small and girlish in the bed, innocent and uninvolved. Her perfume lay on the quiet air. So get out, he told himself. Pack and check out. The job here is done, so why stay? You know where the trip wire is, so back off. Your luck is still running good. Good? Let's call it just fair. But a good knock is in order, for the steady nerves, the morale of the hatchetman. He went slowly to the end of the corridor and walked into the suite. Bobby Fayhouser put a magazine aside and stood up. "Hi, Floyd! They've all gone down to dinner. Almost all of them."

Hubbard nodded and went to the bar. He made himself a heavy highball. "To conventions," he said. "To jackasses."

"That's a toast to the whole human race, isn't it?"

"Cynicism is a privilege of the very young, Robert. Now that I'm older, I'm becoming one of the boys, earnest and folksy."

"Are you sore about something?"

"Nothing terribly specific, I guess. Keep it to yourself, Bobby, but I am departing. This large knock and the one to follow are in the nature of farewell toasts."

"Are you figuring on getting smashed? I mean, it's none of my business, but I thought you'd play it cool all the way, Mr. Hubbard. But I guess, if you're going, you can chug-a-lug a few. I guess you wouldn't have wanted to get too loose in front of everybody while you still . . . you still had work to do."

"So good reports would go back?"

"I guess so."

Hubbard finished the drink and dropped another cube in the glass and picked up the bottle. "Let's just say that suddenly I've become highly nervous, Bobby. I'm so nervous I'm forgetting to be smart. I've got an un-used gift certificate. Everybody reads my mail. I hit white-haired ladies between the eyes. My sunburn itches. I'm stronger than I would want to be, given the choice. I didn't take a very good shower this evening. When the world is turning, you should be able to run fast enough to stay in the same place."

Fayhouser looked slightly alarmed. "You lose me with no trouble, sir."

"Losing myself comes next. Cheers."

"Excuse me and all that, but you're setting a pace. Thirty minutes you might last. Take it out of gear right now, Mr. Hubbard, and you could coast quite a way."

Hubbard smiled at him. "You are so right, Bobby. I should coast, shouldn't I? If I pass out, I can't do the damage. I have to be able to keep walking and talking, or I'll skip my chance to become a figure of fun. My God, you should have seen good old Floyd Hubbard at that convention!"

Fayhouser said, "Don't get me wrong in the way I mean this, Floyd, but is there anything I can do?"

Hubbard put the empty glass down. The decorator colors were brighter. His lips felt rubbery. "You are a good man, Fayhouser. Keep your head down for a while. Keep the knees slightly bent, feet apart, open stance, slow backswing."

"I don't play. I'm only a caddy."

"And I used to be on the house committee," Hub-bard said, and walked out of the suite. He went down to one of the hotel bars and drank the world a little mistier, right to the place where he could find his drink-ing grin, and his drinking uninvolvement, and walk slow-ly among the people, delighted by all things, but wary of the little edges of tears or panic or violence which, unless carefully watched, could move in and bust the holiday balloon in his chest. Time changed to bottle time, running raggedly, fast and slow, and the world became an inexpert hobby film, alternating vividness with blank frames, with a tilt to the camera and the focus unreliable.

After a time when the film was blank, he was in a corridor, edged into a corner, alone with Dave Daniels and being breathed upon by him.

"Get cute again, kiddo. Go ahead."

"I'm terribly cute," Hubbard said, and suddenly he had the corridor rug against his cheek, and he was articulating each suck of air. Daniels helped him up, and Hubbard felt a wild delight. "We could fight," he said, still gasping. "Let's find a place."

"Shut up! I'm asking you again. Where's that slut?"

"Have you been asking me?"

"Where's Cory? Don't horse with me, Hubbard."

"Cory? Dave, boy, she doesn't like you."

"She likes me fine. She just doesn't know it yet."

"Aren't we going to fight, Dave?"

"Later."

"Is that a promise?"

"Yes."

"If I tell you where she is, we'll go someplace? And fight it out?"

"We sure will, Hubbard."

He took keys out of his pocket. It took him a long time to sort them. After he gave Daniels the key to 847, the only key he had left was the one to 1102. It seemed a hell of a thing that it should take so long to sort out just two keys. He looked up to share this ludicrous joke with Daniels, but he found himself alone in the corridor. He shrugged. He listened. He heard laughter and music and the rumble of conversation from the rooms down the hall. He headed, smiling, toward the party sounds.

Again time took a tilt, a lurch, and when the image cleared he was in the crowded parlor of a smaller, unfamiliar suite, sitting in a straight chair pulled close to a corner couch, leaning forward, grinning, talking to one of the Honey-Bunny blondes, talking so intently about something so important that it slid out of his mind the moment this increase of awareness came upon him.

She sat slumped, flaccid and dull-eyed and slightly drunk, looking through him and beyond him. Close beside her, in the same slack, reclining posture was a man Hubbard did not know, a narrow man with a bandaged eye and shiny black hair. Honey-Bunny wore a pink, fanciful dinner dress, taut across her thighs. The man had his good eye closed, and a drink in his free hand. With his other hand he gently stroked the satiny thigh in the absent-minded way a man might stroke a dog. His head was turned toward the girl, and he spoke in a droning constant murmur which Hubbard could not understand. Each time he began to be too bold, the girl would pick his hand up by the wrist and drop it away from her.

Hubbard very cautiously, very carefully, checked the aspects of this new reality, feeling that if he was too brisk about it, it would all merge and flow away from him and he would find himself instantly in some other place and time. He turned. The room was full, and most everyone was standing, laughing, yelping above the blare of music. He saw Charlie Gromer and Stu Gallard and Cass Beatty, but he did not know any of the rest of them. He found a half cup of black coffee in his hand. He sipped it. It was tepid, and too sweet, but he could not taste liquor in it. His tie was loosened, his collar open, and his knee was damp where something had spilled and nearly dried. He looked at his watch and saw that it was twenty minutes of ten, and wondered if he had had anything at all to eat.

He looked at the slack, young, disinterested face of the girl and leaned closer and said, "What was I saying?"

"What?"

"What were we talking about?"

She focused on him with apparent effort, yawned and said, "I wooden know. You were talking and talking. Who listens?"

"Who listens?" said the stranger with the bandaged eye.

Hubbard's stomach felt sore. He pressed the soreness and remembered Dave Daniels, the looming size of him, the leathery equine face, the soured breath, the torso that looked as if it had been built of raw timbers and scrap metal. He marveled for a moment at his own idiocy in actually wanting to try to fight a beast like that. Then a pure terror came into his mind, like a silent white explosion. He started to spring up out of the chair, believing for one deadly moment that he had given Daniels the key to a room where Jan was, where she slept defenseless in the darkness. And then he remembered that Jan was far away, and Cory was in the room. He settled back into the chair and drank the coffee and put the cup on the floor. He told himself there was never any such person as the Cory of the night wind, the sea wind on the flat roof over the cabanas. She had never been. There was only Cory-whore, who could handle Daniels.

He told himself it did not matter, not to him, or Cory, or Daniels. It was an incident at a convention. Conventions were thickets of incidence and accident. So he smiled in a rather rigid way at the Honey-Bunny blonde, and tried to think of something that might make her laugh and be happy. Water started to run out of his eyes, for no reason. He blinked rapidly but it would not stop. In his teary and distorted vision he saw her face change, saw it quicken with interest and a tender concern. She sat up so she could reach him, cupped her palm against his cheek and said, "Hey now! Hey now, mister!"

"I . . I can't make it stop," he said.

"It's real bad, isn't it?"

"There's nothing wrong. Really, there's nothing wrong at all," he said, and stood up, turned to the door, stumbled once, and made his way through the sound and the people and out into the corridor, and was astonished to find himself still on the eighth floor, and only a couple of doors away from the hospitality suite. He started slowly down the corridor toward the elevators.

The Honey-Bunny startled him when she took his arm. He stopped and leaned against the wall and, to his own vast annoyance, snuffled like a child. She stood close in front of him and dabbed at his face with a tissue from her purse, musky with her perfume.

"It happens to me, honest," she said. "All of a sudden for no damn reason. Honest to God, seeing it happen to you, my heart all of a sudden turned over, you know?"

"It's just from drinking. It's a crying jag."

"But you're not drunk enough for that, sweetheart. You were talking fine. Gee, you still can't stop, can you?"

"No. I can't seem to stop."

"You got a room here?"

He remembered the other key. He had forgotten the number. He took it out of his pocket. She found it from him and took his arm again and steered him to the elevators.

"This is idiotic," he said.

"Don't try to talk about it or think about it or feel sorry for it."

They went up to eleven, and walked an incredible distance, and got lost once. She opened the room, and bolted the door after they were inside. She made murmurous sounds of comfort, eased him out of his jacket and made him lie down on one of the beds. She brought a small cold towel and folded it and laid it across his eyes, then unlaced his shoes and took them off.

He felt the bed tilt and settle slightly, and knew she was sitting on the edge of the bed. She took his hand.

"Better?" she asked.

"I think so."

"What's your name, dear?"

"Floyd. Floyd Hubbard."

"Don't feel bad about bawling. A man should be able to cry, you know? Hughie, the son of a bitch, couldn't cry a drop unless maybe a horse runs out of money for him. That I should have known before I married him."

"You're the married one."

"Yeah. Honey, with the mole. He's on a gig in Jax."

"What?"

"He's playing in Jacksonville. Two weeks to go."

There was a long silence. "What's it like," she asked, "when the tears come? What are you thinking?"

"It hasn't happened since I was a kid, Honey."

"But what were you thinking?"

"I . . . I don't know. As if . . . everything was moving away from me, and I couldn't get hold of anything any more. As if I'd never really known anybody and never would know anybody, all my life."

"Yes," she breathed. "Yes, it's like that, isn't it? When there's no way to get close enough, and you wait and wait for wonderful things that are never going to happen. Floyd. Floyd, sweetheart?" She took the towel from his eyes, moved so she was looking down at him. "Look, I don't mess around. You understand that?"

"Yes."

"People get enough wrong ideas already, the business we're in."

"I can see how that might be."

"But if you want me . . . right now this time it's okay."

"I don't know if I can even . . ."

"So who cares? Mostly it's just to hold you, that's all. Somebody for both of us to hold, okay?"

She left a single lamp burning on a far table and draped it with a bath towel. She undressed and came to the bed and undressed him as gently and impersonally as if he were a drowsy child. He climbed under the sheet and blanket, and she came in beside him and sighed, and took him into the warm abundance of her arms, and hitched about until she could nest his head against her breasts. When, more out of a sense of duty than out of desire, he started to caress her, she said, in a murmurous whisper, "Don't, sweetheart. Just you lie quiet. If it has to happen, we'll let it happen, and if doesn't, that's all right too. We're both so damn tired. You know it? Tired of a million things."

He drifted off and awakened and drifted off again and when he awakened again, he wanted her, but in a quiet, unemphatic way. It went easily, and it was drowsy and unreal, and not very important. There was the strong, steady, docile movement of her and, far away from him and below him, like something at the foot of a dark stairwell, a recurrent arcing and glimmering of specific sensation which neither diminished nor increased until finally she quickened, and became very strong, and, as she brought it about, sobbed once, sighed several times, and sweetly slowed to rest.

"Somebody close," she said in a sighing voice, "to hold."

"I know."

"It was kinda sweet."

"Yes."

"Stay just like this, please, for a while."

The phone began to ring.

Nine

AS soon as Dave Daniels came sagging back down out of the wildness, back to awareness of himself, back to the ability to identify this time, this place and this woman beneath him, he pushed himself away from her and stood up in the dark room, his heart still hammering, his breathing still ragged.

He squatted and fumbled at his discarded clothing and found his cigarettes and lighter. He lit a cigarette and walked to the terrace door, slid it open and stepped out onto the tiny triangular terrace. There was a slight breeze in the humid night, and it felt more pleasant against his sweaty flesh than had the air conditioning in the room behind him, where the woman lay.

He perched one hip on the rough texture of the concrete wall and, as the heart beat ever less rapidly, he looked at another angle of the hotel, at the few rooms where he could see in, where people moved and talked in their little bright boxes. It made him feel remote, wise and powerful to be naked and unseen in the darkness and look at people who could not know he was there. Below him were the areas of brightness and shadow, tinted spots on the palm trunks, twisted shadows of tropical plantings, the bright outlines of the lighted pools. He heard the merged sounds of many kinds of music and the gutturals of the sea and the constant soft alto of city traffic, pierced by a yap of car horn, a far siren, a woman's bright tipsy laugh from the shadows far below him.

He knew he was still a little bit drunk, but not very much, because the prolonged strenuous taking of the woman had boiled it out of his blood. He felt tired, calm, wise and agreeably wicked. The bitch had been a disappointment. After fighting him so explosively, she had been stubbornly inert, but he had built himself to such a peak of wanting her that her reactions were not truly important.

Daniels scores again, he thought. Daniels never misses. Sometimes it is damned close to what they call rape, but they usually find out it's exactly what they want. Twice it didn't work out just right and it was expensive to settle it quietly. But not with this one. Not with a girl on call.

He snapped his cigarette out into the night and went back into the room, half expecting her to have gone into the bathroom, but she was as he had left her, tumbled and spread diagonally across the foot of the bed she had been in when he had come into the room, her head over the edge. He could just make her out in the small light that filtered into the room.

He stood near the foot of the bed and said, "You're not that worn out, cutie."

He reached down to touch her in a hearty, familiar, casual way, put his hand against flesh, snatched it away, backed slowly until his shoulders touched the wall. He stood there breathing through jaws held wide.

After a long time he found the energy to go draw the draperies and turn a single floor lamp on and look at her. "But I didn't hit you that hard!" he whispered. "You shouldn't have got loose and run for the door. You shouldn't have done that, damn you!"

He wanted a drink desperately, and at the same time was glad there was no liquor in the room, because he knew he was going to have to start thinking very soon, thinking with great care and caution. Because now, unless he was very careful, everything could go whirling down the drain. He wanted to cover the body so he could stop looking at it, but he knew he should take no meaningless action. It was like being in a pit with a poisonous snake. If you moved perfectly, you were home free. If you did the smallest thing wrong, you were dead.

He went into the bathroom, turned on the cold white blaze of fluorescence, filled the basin with cold water and sloshed his face and head, snorting and snuffling. As he dried himself, he remembered the night bolt on the room door and fixed it.

After making certain there was no gap in the closure of the draperies, he turned on every light in the room. He paced back and forth, glancing at the body, accustoming himself to it, because he knew he would have to touch it sooner or later. He hummed to himself. He beat his fist into his palm. He cheered himself by thinking, I have been in a hundred jams. I have gotten out of every one. I can get out of this one.

He sat on the other bed, facing her, and her upside-down face was close enough to touch, her eyes partially open. He got up quickly and checked the room for her possessions, found clothes, purse, swimsuit, bathing cap.

The big limiting factor was how much Floyd Hubbard might remember. There was too good a chance he would remember giving the room key to Daniels. That seemed to eliminate the chance of leaving her just as she was, or dressing her and dumping her over the edge of the terrace railing.

He hit himself over the ear with his clenched fist, shook his head violently, and went over it again. Any look of murder would result in a more careful investigation than he could stand. There was a subtle, sickening exaggeration to the angle of her head. The backhand blow had snapped her neck just before he had caught her up and tumbled her back onto the foot of the bed. There was a faint blue bruise on the delicate line of her jaw.

He looked at his upper arm, near his shoulder, at the three deep parallel gouges her nails had made as she had gotten away from him the second time. They could check the meat and blood under her nails, type it.

The plan was vague at first, but as he went over it in his mind it became ever more specific. The single crucial factor was the night bolt and chain. He turned all the lights off and went out onto the terrace again. The vertical sawtooth construction made it impossible to reach the terraces to the right or the left. When he was certain he was not being watched by anyone, he stepped over the railing, stood on a narrow edge of concrete, crouched and, holding onto the railing, looked down onto the terrace directly below. The room was dark. It would be a simple matter to lower himself, hang from the edge on which he stood, swing in and drop onto the terrace below. He had always been a good athlete. He trusted his body to perform as he wanted it to, without fear or hesitation. It was unlikely that the terrace door below would be locked on the inside. It could be forced if it was. And if the room was empty, or if people were asleep there, in either case he would go quickly and quietly through the room and out into the seventh floor corridor.

He went back into 847 and turned the lights back on. He wiped his hands on his thighs several times before he could force himself to touch the small body, so eerily still, so oddly flattened. Once he had begun, he worked steadily and quietly.

He did not know how long it took. When it was done, he tried to look at the scene the way a policeman might. They would have had to use nippers on the night chain. They would find both beds neatly made, her clothing laid out on one of them. They would find one lamp on in the bedroom, and the room key on the desk. They would hear the sound of the shower, and when they opened the bathroom door they would find her sprawled halfway out of the shower, the glass shower door open. She would have her swim cap on, and she would be belly down across the raised sill of the shower stall, the damp cake of soap inches from her outstretched hand. (And they would not guess how he had gagged as he had cleaned the nails of that outstretched hand.)

Because they would have to cut the chain to get in, they would not be suspicious. And he knew he could not take the risk of leaving by way of the room door. He had not been seen entering, he knew.

He dressed quickly, put one shoe in each side pocket of his jacket, took a long, slow look around, then went through the orange-yellow draperies and out onto the terrace and eased the glass door shut behind him. He was glad to see that very little light came through the draperies—not enough to silhouette him in any dangerous fashion.

Once again he looked for a long time in all possible directions. He could not see down into the shadows of the pool area. Somebody could be down there, staring up at the sky. It was a risk he would have to take, a minor one compared to all the others.

When he was quite ready, he rehearsed in his mind the moves he would make. He straddled the railing, found the small edge with his stocking foot, swung the other leg over and crouched as before. The terrace wall was pierced with ornamental holes which provided safe, sturdy hand-holds. When his hands were secure, fingers locked on the inner edge of two of the lower holes, he lowered himself carefully until he was extended at full length, his legs dangling. It brought his eyes below the level of the cantilevered slab which formed the deck of his own terrace, the one he was leaving. The railing of the terrace below was about a foot below his toes. He decided that rather than risk the noise of swinging in and dropping, he would be able to reach the railing with his toes if he took a second hand-hold on the narrow edge on which he had previously braced his feet. He brought his left hand down first, clamping his fingertips on the edge, then slowly transferred his weight to his left arm. The strain on his fingertips of his left hand was great, but he knew he could endure it for the small part of a second it would take to slide his right hand down to the same small edge, and then his toes would reach the lower railing.

In the instant he let go with his right hand, he felt the small edge crumbling under the fingers of his left hand, powdering away. He spasmed his body inward, dropped the few remaining inches and landed on the railing, in precarious balance for one moment of triumph and gladness, and then he was tilting back, flailing his arms, barking the skin off his knuckles on the cement overhead. As he knew he was going, he tried to squat and catch the edge of the railing he was on, but all he was able to do was flick his fingertips against the outer edge of it. He went down, and all the lights were going around him in a huge slow wheeling. He filled his lungs with the moist air that was rushing by his face and gave a great despairing roar which ended when the small of his back smashed the ornamental iron fence which separated the pool area from one of the service areas. A woman began a metronomic screaming, becoming perceptibly more hoarse with each earnest effort.

Alan Amory, the Public Relations Director of the Sultana Hotel, walked behind the bar of the Hideaway Club to make a drink for fat Captain Brewhane of Homicide, the last arrival. It was after midnight. All lights were on in the office suite, all draperies closed. Amory had the feeling it was going rather well, better than he had expected at first. There was a special protocol about these matters whenever a major hotel was involved, particularly in a resort area. The problems were delicate. You had to be particularly careful about the way things were said. Any hint of challenge had to be avoided at all costs.

One small victory had been gained already. He had stalled the members of the working press beyond the final moment for any possible inclusion in the morning papers. So, unless it turned out truly gaudy, there would be a patina of staleness which would limit coverage in the afternoon papers tomorrow.

He carried the drink back toward the quiet mumbling of male conversations at the big table in the rear of the small club room. When he put the drink in front of Brewhane, they all looked up at him. They wore the mild little smiles of poker players: Brewhane, Detective Lieutenant Al Farrier, Rick DiLarra—the convention director for the Sultana, Detective-Sergeant Milton Manning, Rice Emper, legal counsel for the hotel and Peter Lipe, an assistant state's attorney.

Amory said, "If you gentlemen will excuse me a moment, the people in my office could be getting impatient. I don't want them leaving. The reporters are camped out in the shrubbery."

"Who have you got?" Brewhane demanded.

"A Mr. Frick. He's the one who . . ."

"Friend of mine," Al Farrier interrupted. "Bill, he's the one called me early about helping him out with the drunk who fell into the courtyard."

"Too bad you couldn't have come around earlier," Brewhane said.

"When I got here at ten we couldn't find him. Fred Frick and I looked every place for the guy."

"Who else?" Brewhane asked.

"A Mr. Mulaney, the dead man's employer. Mr. Hubbard, who has the room where the woman's body was found. And a Mrs. Hugh Constanto, a . . . friend of Mr. Hubbard."

"Go tell them I want them to stay put, and come right back, Amory," Brewhane directed.

Amory went to his office. Frick and Mulaney sat on a leather couch talking in low tones. Hubbard sat on a straight chair, leaning on his knees, his head lowered.

Honey Constanto sat in a deep leather chair, looking half asleep.

"You'll have to stay around a little while longer," Amory said. "I'm sorry."

Frick said, "Sure." Mulaney nodded. The other two gave no word or gesture.

Amory went back to the club room and joined the group at the table. He spoke before anyone could speak to him, taking that chance to make a point in a rather oblique way. "Thank God we were able to get Daniels' body out as quietly as we did. I don't think there's fifteen guests in the hotel who have any inkling anything like that happened. The girl was less of a problem, of course We've had deaths in rooms before. We have a standard operating procedure for that, and we got the usual fine cooperation from the medical examiner, from the ambulance people and from your men, Captain."

Brewhane said, impatiently, "Let's recap this thing and find out which way we're going. Catch me up if I'm wrong on the broad picture, Al. You were here hunting for that guy when he squashed himself in the courtyard. Milt, here, was with you. Both of you off duty, doing a favor for a friend. So while the body was being hustled away so it could be examined down at the police morgue, you started trying to find out where it fell from. In that process, you came across that room with the door chained and no answer. And that's where you found the body of the Barlund woman."

Rice Emper interrupted smoothly, saying, "But I think we should be careful not to jump to the conclusion that Daniels fell or jumped from the terrace of 847. There were convention parties going on in at least a dozen rooms on the sixth, seventh, eighth, ninth and tenth floors overlooking the area where Daniels landed. We know he was so recklessly drunk that Mr. Frick asked his old friend here, Al Farrier, to come and help out, for Daniels' own good. All of those rooms have terraces. He could have gone out on any one of them, feeling sick and dizzy . . ."

The young assistant state's attorney, Peter Lipe, cleared his throat and said, "I suppose 847 could be checked carefully for . . . for any clue that that's where Daniels was. Fingerprints or something like that."

Brewhane glared at him. "When and if you get a file

on this, Lipe, then you complain if you don't like it. But don't tell me how to make it up."

"But if people were looking for Daniels and couldn't find him . . ."

Brewhane leaned back in his chair, ignoring Lipe. With his eyes half shut he said, "I suppose if we didn't have too much to do, and we weren't short of men and time, we could make a hell of a lot of fuss about this. We know Daniels was in 847 sometime during the evening. . . . Correction—we know he *could* have been in 847, because somebody told you, Al, they had given him the key."

"Hubbard told me about ten times. He was shook," Al said.

"But," Brewhane continued, "we could rush around trying to add up two and two and get nine and create a hell of a lot of stir and confusion and find out in the end we just didn't have enough to go on, and all we would succeed in doing is hurting a lot of people for no good reason. We could jump too fast at little things like Daniels not wearing his shoes, and the fresh gouges on his shoulder, and the woman's shower cap being on backwards, and come up with some cute theory about Daniels killing her and making it look like a shower-bath accident, and then trying to leave by way of the terrace and slipping." He turned to give Amory a prolonged, sleepy stare. "And even though we might get no place at all checking all that out, Amory, we might have to go through the motions if somebody agitates us to keep looking."

Amory glanced sidelong at Emper, and knew this was the crucial moment. He tried to keep his tension hidden. "Mr. Daniels was a Chicago sales executive, Captain. All his friends were disturbed about his heavy drinking. Mr. Mulaney told me that Mrs. Daniels was also very upset about it. By the way, Mr. Mulaney phoned her from my office long distance and broke the terrible news to her. He said she seemed stunned, but at the same time she acted as if she'd expected something like this to happen. And certainly Mr. Daniels' employers are not going to want to pursue this any further. I'm sure the company would be most happy to have it all handled as quietly as possible. Mr. Frick suddenly remembered Daniels complaining about feeling dizzy and nauseated earlier in the evening. I've always felt those terrace railings were a little too low, actually."

Brewhane nodded. "But the woman is local. That could be something else again, couldn't it?"

Amory spoke slowly, selecting his wording with extreme care. "I took the liberty of helping Lieutenant Farrier check her out, Captain. She was working on a freelance magazine assignment. She was a divorcée, living alone."

"Next of kin?"

"I took the liberty of making a phone call, with Lt. Farrier's permission. I called a woman I had reason to believe might know her. A Mrs. Alma Bender."

The Captain's eyes widened. "Well, well, well," he said softly.

"Mrs. Bender says that as far as she knows there's no next of kin close enough to have any particular interest in the Barlund woman, dead or alive. Mrs. Bender says that the Barlund woman was only a casual acquaintance, but that she would be willing to . . . take over the arrangements for burial and so forth, *provided* it's just a routine case of accidental death. Because she was only an acquaintance, Mrs. Bender doesn't feel that she should get involved in anything which might get too much attention in the papers. She might not even be able to identify the body, if that's the case. She's waiting to hear."

Brewhane looked at Alan Amory with a small gleam of humor. "Because of this relationship with Alma Bender, which you just *happen* to know about, Amory, would you care to make any guess about motive—if we got all carried away?"

Amory swallowed. "I don't know what to say. It wouldn't be robbery. Mr. Daniels was a successful man. And it could hardly be a rape murder, could it?"

Detective Farrier said, "The thing is, Bill, nobody is going to push."

Peter Lipe spoke in a young, petulant voice. "It's all very neat, isn't it? You don't even *want* to find out what actually happened, Captain, do you? Maybe somebody on the newspapers will be a little more anxious to add your two and two and see what . . ."

"We can go into it very thoroughly, young man," Captain Brewhane said.

Amory had the horrid feeling that Lipe had spoiled it all. Rice Emper smiled and said, "You seem to be accusing Captain Brewhane of incompetence, Mr Lipe. There's a formal procedure you can follow, you know. Before you embark on anything so   so very dangerous, I suggest you take it up with your superior, John Swazey I have every confidence he will give you sound advice. He is one of my oldest and closest friends."

"All I meant was . . ."

"Nobody on any newspaper is going to get eager," Amory said. "I kid you not. They know it wouldn't get into print. Big hotels do too much advertising, Mr. Lipe. We do a hell of a lot more local advertising than makes sense—except in situations like this."

"In a big hotel like this one," Sergeant Milton Manning said in a heavy self-conscious voice, "the way I see it, you got two accidental deaths in one night, right? So it's only natural to try to tie them up in one package, and there's maybe twenty ways you could try to do it, but where the hell would you be even if it worked? Who gets jailed? Daniels has kids and a wife. Hubbard has got a wife and kids. He's in the clear because he was sacked up with the blonde broad while whatever was going on was going on, but he would have to be brought into it on account of the key. So you end up with a hell of a lot of fuss and heartbreak over one dead flooze. That's the way I see it. And, like the Captain said, maybe after all the fireworks, we can't get any place anyway, after filling up the newspapers all over the country."

Rick DiLarra cleared his throat and said uncertainly, "I may have made a terrible mistake. I really didn't know there was any chance of it turning into some kind of an investigation. You see, I've had Mr. Hubbard's things moved to a different room, and I had the woman's things packed and sent down to the police morgue, and I told the housekeeper on eight to get some maids and clean up 847. I . . . I suppose they're done by now."

Amory managed to keep his sigh from being audible. He knew it was over. He knew by the expression on Captain Brewhane's face. The Captain stood up and said, "We don't have to go any further with this. I see no connection between the two accidental deaths. Amory, let's go make a verbal statement to those reporters out there. Al, you go talk to your friend Frick and the others, tell them they're free to go and put the fear of God into them about giving any interviews. Thanks for the drink and the cooperation, gentlemen."

Hubbard looked up when Al Farrier walked into the office. Farrier was a burly man with small delicate features. He paused just inside the door and relighted a cigar and grinned at them.

"What's the word, Al?" Fred Frick asked eagerly.

"Everything is all settled down nice. We got an accidental on both of them, and with the report I'll write, the confirmation is automatic."

"I gave him the key," Hubbard said in a hopeless voice.

"So what? So maybe he used it. Maybe he didn't. The thing is, she borrowed your room to get cleaned up, right? Twenty thousand people a year fall and kill themselves in bathrooms. It isn't an unusual thing. And it's all figured out that he couldn't have landed where he did if he came off the terrace of 847."

"What?" Hubbard asked. "What was that?"

"You don't come into it in any way, Mister," Farrier said.

"But I . . ."

"Shut up," the blonde girl said. "Leave it alone. Honest to God, Floyd, for hours and hours you've been trying to put your ass in a sling. You want trouble? I sure don't. I don't want any part of anything. I want to go home. So kindly keep your fat mouth shut."

"That's a smart girl talking," Fred said. "We all should leave it just the way it is. Right, Jesse?"

"Absolutely," Jesse Mulaney said.

"Now all of you get one thing squared away," Farrier said. "And this includes you, Fred. Anybody asks questions about this, you three men have been questioned on account of being with the same company as Daniels. Beyond that, you know nothing."

"So what am I doing here?" the girl demanded. "I was with Floyd, that's all. And I won't make a mistake like that again in a hurry." She stood up, gave a hitch to her pink dress and said, "I'm walking right out of here right now."

"Go ahead, darling," Farrier said.

She looked at him blankly. "Huh?"

"Goodnight and good luck."

She hesitated one more moment and then walked out.

When they went out into the larger office, DiLarra was there, waiting for Hubbard. They went together to the main desk. DiLarra apologized for any inconvenience, told him his things had been moved to a new room, and gave him a key to 609, in the south wing.

Floyd Hubbard went to his new room. It was one-fifteen in the morning. His possessions were in good order. He had a headache. His eyes felt sandy, and his mouth tasted vile. He sat on the bed. He felt too dispirited to make the first effort toward undressing and going to bed.

After a long time there was a knock on the door. He let Jesse Mulaney in. Jesse looked big and ancient and dog tired.

"We better go over this some," Jesse said.

"Sit down."

Jessie sat in the armchair. Hubbard sat on the bed, facing him. They did not look directly at each other, except in fleeting glances, and never at the same instant.

"I talked to Fred," Jesse said. "And Cass Beatty and Connie. It won't look good to keep on being jolly for the two days left. I gave orders to close the suite. We'll keep the exhibit going, without the twins. Dave was a pretty good boy. It wouldn't look right to keep on with it, not this year. We'll go to New York tomorrow, and I'll go to the funeral in Chicago."

"Do you want me to tell you it's a good plan?"

"I just thought you'd like to know how things are."

"It would be nice to find out how things are. I wish I could find out."

Jesse stirred in the chair, recrossed his legs. "I can understand how this hit you hard, Floyd boy. I guess you got pretty close to that pretty little girl in a short time. Hard to imagine her dead all of a sudden."

Hubbard looked listlessly at the older man, feeling no animosity. "She told me you and Fred hired her to make a damn fool of me. It would have worked, Jesse, up to a point. I mean, she would have pulled something obvious enough in some place where enough people would have seen it. But it wouldn't have made any difference in the recommendation I'll make on you."

He watched Mulaney, expecting protestations of innocence. Mulaney sighed and loosened the knot of his vivid tie and said, "It was a lousy idea, I guess."

"It certainly was."

"When things start to go wrong, I guess your ideas get worse and worse. Funny she told you, though."

"She wasn't well. She wasn't reliable."

"I'm not trying to duck it, Floyd boy, but it was Fred's idea to start with. And ever since I told him to go ahead with it, I've felt ashamed. But I wasn't going to call it off. I have to tell you that. I fired Fred tonight. He's always been like a part of me walking around, the part I don't like very much. That's why I've been nicer to him all these years than I would have been—if I couldn't see part of me in him. Do you understand that?"

"Yes."

"He cried like a little kid. He said it wouldn't save my job for me, by firing him. I said I didn't mean for it to. I said I wanted to fire him before they take away my authority to fire anybody. I told him I wanted that chance. But I guess I was punishing myself."

"I wouldn't know about that."

"Connie told me what you said about me. You didn't have to say that to her. You could have said it to me."

"I'm ashamed I said it to her, Jesse. I'm sorry."

"I don't think you told her anything she didn't know. But I think she knows some things you don't know. They aren't the kind of things that you'd look for in a sales manager, but I have the idea they're worth something."

Hubbard stared down at the floor and said, "Did we kill her, Jesse? Did we kill Cory? You and me and Fred Frick?"

"She fell while she was taking a shower."

"Daniels was after her."

"And he beat it out of Fred, what the actual deal was. Funny how happy Connie was about me firing Fred. I can't get it out of my mind. I knew she didn't like him very much, but I didn't know she felt that way."

"Jesse, I keep wondering what would have happened if I'd refused to tell Daniels anything about Cory."

"I guess he would have knocked you down, taken your room key and gone looking to see if she was in your room."

"That's the salesman's knack, isn't it? You tell people what they want most to hear."

"You know what she was, boy. So she took Dave on and sent him on his way and then took a shower. What's one more guy to one of those girls?"

"You're a great salesman, Jesse."

Jesse leaned forward. "One idea I wish I could sell you. But now you've got more reason than ever to throw me out. You've got a good personal reason now. I could stay out of the way for two years. I mean just hold the job and not get in anybody's way. I'd even draw no pay, but nobody would have to know that. Just to keep the name, boy, until my time is up."

"Isn't there any threat to go with it?"

Jesse shrugged. "There'll be rumors. I can't stop them. Fred found you in the sack with one of the twins from our exhibit. You and Daniels were squabbling over a little whore before he fell off the hotel. You were walking around pretty tight tonight. A lot of people saw that."

"You can't stop them, but you could build them up a little."

"I didn't say that, now did I?"

Hubbard sat quietly and felt as if a hollow place in the middle of his chest was slowly filling up with molten metal, solidifying, turning at last to something so rigid and enduring it would last him all his life and serve him well. It would be there whenever he needed it. Jan would not have to know it was there. She needed no knowledge of the implacable, the merciless.

He stood up and said quietly, "What makes you think rumors like that could hurt me, you silly son of a bitch? You know how the rumors will level out. They'll know all over the industry you tried to job me and got out-maneuvered. And they'll have the idea I got to have my cake and eat it too. She was very good, Jesse. Very very good. Thanks for picking up the tab. The other one was nice too. I'm going to phone John Camplin. You can stay and listen, or you can leave now. It doesn't matter to me what you do."

When Mulaney did not move, he went around the bed and placed a call to Houston, to John Camplin's unlisted home phone.

"Sorry to call at such an hour, John, but we've had a tragedy here, and Mulaney is folding the tent on most of the AGM contingent, so I'll fly back tomorrow. The head of the Chicago District, David Daniels, fell over a railing on a terrace on one of the upper floors and was killed. Yes, he'd been drinking heavily, but that won't be played up. No, it's all being handled as quietly as possible. Mulaney informed Mrs. Daniels tonight. As far as I know, there are no problems of liability involved, but I thought you'd like to get advance word on it. What was that? Oh, I'll make a written report with my reasoning in detail, but off the cuff I can tell you that I think we should ask for Mulaney's resignation at the first opportunity. The man is too limited for the job. No, John, I wouldn't advise retaining him in any capacity whatsoever. There's no help he can give us on anything. Sales needs a top to bottom housecleaning just as soon as the new man can get his feet on the ground. Okay. I haven't made reservations yet. When I do I'll wire Jan and have her phone in my ETA . . . No, I'm completely sold on conventions, John. I've been wallowing in bourbon and broads twenty-four hours a day. Nothing like it anywhere. See you tomorrow. 'Night, John."

After he hung up he waited a few moments before turning to look at Mulaney. Mulaney was standing. He wore a strange shy smile, curiously boyish. It was a smile to go with a blush, but Mulaney's face was a ghastly gray-white under the red webs of the broken veins.

"I guess that does it," Jesse Mulaney said, moving quite slowly toward the door.

"Wait a minute, Jesse. Think of the other ways I could have done it. I could have asked you to leave before I made the call. Or, talking to Camplin, I could have played it to you, then called him back later and given it to him the way I just did. What the hell good does it do *anybody* to keep hope alive when there's no hope at all? No matter what you tried to do to me, or if you'd done nothing at all to me, it would have been exactly the same."

Mulaney frowned. "How did things get so far ahead of me? Maybe it's all because I never could really believe in all that new stuff, son. All the cards with the little holes. All the crap about surveys and images. Limited. That's what you told Camplin I am. When I was eighteen years old I sold a Cherokee Indian a solid gold fountain pen for twenty-eight dollars. It was a used pen and it had the wrong initials on it, and I'd bought it at a streetcar company auction of stuff people had lost and hadn't

claimed. I bought it for eleven dollars, and you know
something? That Indian couldn't write. He was going to
use it to sign his X."

"Would you rather have been kidded along about this,
Jesse?"

The big man rubbed his eyes. "The way I feel now,
maybe. I guess I break stuff to myself a little at a time."
He moved closer to the door and turned and said, "Connie
calls you the new people. I've kept telling her the world
and human nature don't change."

"I was given a job to do."

"I can appreciate that. My God, I've fired a lot of men.
Hired a lot of them, fired a lot of them. You know the
big difference between us? Never in my life did I enjoy
firing a man."

"For Chrissake, Mulaney, do you believe I *enjoyed*
this?"

"Didn't you?" Mulaney asked. He grinned and chuckled
and winked, though his eyes looked dead. "Not any?
Not at all? Not a smidgin?" Still chuckling he let himself
out into the hall and closed the door quietly.

After Floyd Hubbard had called the likely airlines and
set up a reservation, he undressed and went into the
bathroom. There he looked at himself with a curiosity
and an intensity he had not used since childhood. He put
his nose close to the mirror and looked into his eyes
until there was nothing left of the world but those staring
brown eyes and a feeling of dizziness.

Entranced, he told himself that nothing could possibly
happen to him that was of any particular importance.
So it did not really matter whether Mulaney had been
right or wrong. He was wrong. There had been no enjoy-
ment. (Forget the conversation with Connie. Forget it
forever.)

So leave us please drop this debilitating introspection.
Personal motivation is academic. The jobs are assigned.
The missions are clear. Be a hammer. Be a blade. Be a
club.

If we need affirmations of existence, slugger, let us
look to the simplified ones, the less bothersome ones—
the command given, the task completed, the money
banked, the new mouth tasted, the new thighs spread,
the new suits fitted, the meat and liquor tasted—all
politely, efficiently, moderately. Measure it all in terms of

salivation, of tastes and juices. Measured that way, it is a short turn around the track, so be the quiet smiler, walk gently, take what you want.

As he went to sleep he reminded himself to get to the airport early enough to have time to select small gifts for Jan and the kids.

Ten

When he checked out of the Sultana at eleven the following morning, the joint convention of COLUDA and NAPATAN was still in full swing. Groups talked in the lobby, and other groups headed toward and away from the committee meetings and the workshops, wearing their badges, interrupting each other with gossip and jokes and industry shoptalk, nursing hangovers or smug with sobriety.

As the cab drove away from the hotel, he glanced back at the welcome banner, and wondered vaguely what banner would replace it. He remembered a phrase from a college course taken long ago. Structured environment. He realized he had acquired a new appraisal of the convention as an institution. It wasn't, as Mulaney seemed to believe, a fun-fest, a week of broads and bottles and letting down the hair. That was a minor part of it. Nor was it a dedication ceremoney, or an educational device.

It was, he decided, an organized way of achieving a gratifying illusion of importance. It was anthropological in nature. It was as if fifty nomad tribes selected a ceremonial meeting place each year, and gathered there to do the ancient ceremonies, elect chiefs, sacrifice maidens, brew bitter remedies, initiate the young men. By gathering in such numbers they could convince themselves they were a great people, who would endure forever. They could make brave speeches to each other about their importance in the frightening size of the universe. They could rattle their symbols of rank, tell the glorious tales of victories since the last time of meeting, and, in quiet corners of the encampment, they could make secret devious plottings, trades, alliances and conspiracies. Thus, at the next convention, AGM should be represented by a cold, taut, canny cadre of men of maximum ability, men who—while remaining suitably affable—would seek

140

out every advantage, every scrap of information, and give nothing away in return, men who would nurse weak drinks, remember names and attend all meetings. He decided to make a special report to John Camplin stating these views.

There was one curious incident during the flight to Houston, an incident which momentarily disturbed him.

He had a window seat in the forward part of the aircraft. After they were en route, he tilted his seat back and cautiously allowed the first memories of Cory to come filtering up into his conscious mind, keeping them at half strength until he became quite certain they would not sting. Superimposed over the fresh memories of her was the first vague outline of his future attitude toward what had happened. He was objective enough to recognize it as a defense device, a rationalization which he could reasonably hope to substantiate. She had been aimed at him like a weapon, and he had had no chance from the beginning.

As he remembered all of it, he felt a vague astonishment that he had been so reluctant to bed her again, so prim and righteous. He felt astonishment and a slight sense of loss. At 26,000 feet, virtue and reluctance seemed asinine.

She had been aimed at him, and she had faked the emotional involvement with the effortlessness of the professional. And she had slipped, fallen and died, which seemed a waste and a shame, but hardly a tragedy. Yet, through taking such a curiously moral stance, he had accidentally made the assuring discovery that the second infidelity diminished the guilt of the first, and that the sum of guilt over two was less than the guilt over one. It might be a little awkward to face Jan this time, but if the formula was consistent, the third would further lessen this middle-class burden of remorse, and by the time he had reached the twentieth, guilt should be reduced to a minor irritation, a psychic hangnail bothersome only when touched. He wished he had been a little more sober when he'd bedded Honey Constanto. She was a little too vague to be a satisfying memory.

Thinking of Honey, he fell asleep. Soon he was in a vast black shower stall, where a luminous liquid fell in heavy drops from the ceiling, like the first rain of a thunderstorm. Cory stood small and naked and smirking in front of him, silvery in the strange light which came from the heavy drops. "You see how it is?" she was saying. "You see how it has to be? And he knew what she was going to do, and tried to scream at her, to beg her not to do it, but he could make no sound. And once she had begun, he could not let himself move, because they had told him that if he moved while she was doing it, it would kill him. He looked down in horror and saw her slide her hands right through the skin and flesh and bone of his chest and felt her hands in there, tugging and turning. "Jan wrote me and told me I had to do it," she said. He felt the thing come loose in his chest and knew she would draw it out and knew he should not look at it, but he could not look away. The luminous rain was falling faster. Cory bit her lip and slowly worked his heart out through the skin, holding it in her cupped hands. He saw it was only a heart, red, wet, shiny and pulsing, and he felt an enormous relief and said, "I could have told you that."

"Don't you see?" she said. "Can't you see what it really is? Can't you see what it's always been, sweetheart?"

And with her thumbs she pressed it, and the thick red membrane broke, and she thumbed it aside. He shouted at her, telling her she was spoiling it, that there was no one around to fix it. He yelled that it was not what Jan wanted her to do, that she was making a mistake. But she thumbed it open, spoiling it, and held it in horrid triumph, and he stared into it and saw, to his utter horror, that the inside of it was . . .

"Hey!" the man beside him said. "Hey, fella!"

Hubbard struggled up out of sleep, sweaty and confused, his heart racing.

"Must of been having a nightmare, the way you were whining and jumping around, fella. You okay?"

"Yes. Thanks. Thanks a lot."

"Bad one?"

"Pretty bad. Yes."

"You should hear my wife get going. She sits up in bed with her eyes wide open and howls like a hound dog. It's a hell of a job waking her up. You woke easy."

Hubbard looked directly at him for the first time and saw a man of his own age, casually dressed, with thinning blond hair and a wide, pleasant, sunburned face.

"I hardly ever dream like that," Hubbard said in apology. "I haven't been getting enough sleep, I guess."

"On vacation?"

"No. Business trip."

"Me too. Checking out some raw land for a possible syndicate operation. Resort housing. Waste of time this trip, though. What's your line?"

The terror and confusion of the dream was still strong in his mind, yet he had begun to be aware of the symbolism of the dream, and it afforded him a sour amusement. "Lately I've been in the business of killing things."

The man looked at him oddly. "You mean like an exterminator?"

"I guess you could call it that."

The man said, uneasily, "It must be an interesting line of work."

"At first it isn't very pleasant. But then one day you realize you're getting used to it, and you wonder if that's really very healthy, but you don't quit because it's a good job and everybody likes the way you do it." He realized he was speaking with too much intensity, but he could not stop. "Finally you get to like it. Do you understand? You get to like it, and then there's no point in quitting, is there? I mean why should a man quit any kind of work he likes?"

"I guess . . . it's a good thing to like your work," the man said, and swallowed, and wiped his mouth on the back of his hand.

"I'm sorry. I was just making a bad joke. I was just kidding around." He knew he had gone too far. He tried to smile reassuringly at the stranger, but the smile was curiously out of control. It kept coming and going, very rapidly. He could feel his mouth twitching with the smile, and he could feel his eyes begin to sting. "I . . I'll tell you what I really do," he said.

"Listen. Don't trouble yourself. Don't bother, fella," the man said. "Just get your rest." He got up hastily and moved up the aisle and picked another seat on the half-empty flight.

It was a full thirty minutes before Floyd Hubbard was able to smile at himself and at the alarmed man.

When you plug along too hard and too long, your nerves get a little unraveled. Like the damn-fool tears last night. But this wasn't as bad as that. And the next time won't be as bad as this. When you know what to expect, you can handle it easier. For a little while he thought of Cory and Honey and Jan, with an equal ration of fondness for each of them, fondness, patience and understanding.

Then he took his dispatch case from under the seat and, using the surface of it as a desk, began to list in longhand the reasons why he felt Jesse Mulaney was inadequate in his job, the list that would form the meat of the typed confidential report he would deliver by hand to John Camplin before the day was over. As he labored to keep it as terse as possible, it made him think of the brevity of the news items he had found in the early edition of the afternoon paper, the one he had bought fifteen minutes before his flight left. Daniels had been given fourteen lines on page nine. Cory had been given twelve lines on page six. In neither case had the hotel been mentioned by name.

Just as he finished, he heard the strident note of the engines change and knew they were beginning to descend for the landing at Houston. He latched his belt, tightened his buttocks, and began the shallow breathing which would bring the plane in safely, time after time.

66-12-3